BITTER TRUTH

SHANNON HOLLINGER

Published By Scene Of The Crime Publishing in 2026

ISBN: 978-1-972098-98-1

This book is dedicated to everyone out there who tries to take care of everything on their own—it's okay to ask for help.

CHAPTER 1

Have you ever had the kind of close call that makes your entire life flash before your eyes? Not me. The second the tiny red dot from the rifle scope catches my eye, and I realize what it is, I'm too busy trying to keep my life than to think about what's already happened during it.

I jump toward the nearest vehicle, hitting the ground, hoping to take shelter. Not even a full second later the window above me shatters, safety glass raining down on me as a resounding crack shatters the silence of the swamp.

My heart feels like it's trying to punch its way out of my chest as I curl into myself, trying to become a smaller target. My breath comes in ragged pants.

"Cassie!" Jake's panicked voice carries through the open doorway where I stood only a moment ago.

"I'm okay." As his shadow darkens the threshold, I add, "Stay inside."

Disbelief that this is happening nudges aside the fear coursing through me. But it is. And as I stare at the exterior of my childhood home, anger that it's happening here, at the sanctuary my grandfather left me, elbows its way through all other feelings to the forefront. How dare—

Two more cracks. Though the doorframe splinters with one of them, I can't see where the other hit. This time I'm the one with terror in my tone. "Jake?"

"I'm fine," he answers.

I draw a deep breath, doing my best to stay calm and steady my nerves. I can't allow emotions to cloud my judgment. The only thing that matters right now is getting Jake and myself through this safely, no matter what it takes. I've got to do something to end this. Fast.

"What can I do?" Jake asks.

"Call Marla and let her know what's happening."

"On it."

My superior officer at the FBI, Director in Charge Marla Jacobson, is a formidable woman. She'll light whatever fire she needs to in order to get the calvary on their way. But she's in Virginia.

The nearest field office to where I am, deep in the heart of the Florida Everglades, is in Miami, almost two hours away. The local sheriff hates me. Which means I'm going to have to handle this, whatever it is, on my own.

Kind of hard when I can't move without revealing myself to the crosshairs. I need to figure out where the shooter is. Until I do, I'm trapped.

Glancing around, I look at what's within reach. There's not much, but as a plan forms, I launch into action.

Dirt wedges under my nails as I use my fingers to rake the pine needles that litter the ground into a pile. My legs tremble as I gather myself into a crouch and fish my keys from my pocket.

Unlocking the door, I slither inside the ancient pickup, squeezing into the passenger side footwell. Sweat makes my palm slick as I reach across the sweltering cab, careful to stay below the dash, and slip the jagged piece of metal into the ignition. Turning it to ACC, I press the cigarette lighter in so it will heat.

The moment it pops out, I grab it and retreat, snatching a few stray receipts on my way as I exit the vehicle. If this works, I never want Jake to give me a hard time for not keeping the car clean again.

Back on the ground, I hold the red-hot coil of the lighter to the edge of one of the papers. Blow gently as the corner starts to wither, until a tiny flame appears. Use it to light my pile of pine needles. Once I have a small fire going, I add the rest of the receipts, the printer paper causing a small cloud of white to appear.

The smoke hangs low and heavy in the humid air. Slowly, it starts to rise. And then I see it—the beam cast by the sniper's red dot sight as it searches for a target.

I follow the direction with my gaze, tracing it to the canopy of an oak on the far side of the driveway, about fifty yards away. Grimace as I find that the gunman is concealed by the thick foliage. Even if I could lay eyes on him, it's a long shot to make with a pistol. But as I pull my firearm from the holster at my back, I tell myself I still have the edge.

They might have the weapon designed for long-distance shooting. An optic to help them aim accurately. A location that they picked for this battle.

But I spent my youth climbing that tree. Did it often enough that there was a time I probably could have scaled it with my eyes closed, relying on muscle memory alone. And as I shut my eyes now, recalling every branch and bough big enough to support the weight of an adult, I know where they must be.

I double-check the angle the reticle is coming from. Aim. Fire three times in quick succession. And get rewarded by a crash as the sniper falls from the tree.

"Those were your shots, right?" Jake's voice sounds closer with each word. His spooked eyes meet mine as he appears through the open doorway, his cell clutched in one hand, a shotgun in the other.

There's no explaining the grief I feel at the sight. At the knowledge that I've brought this trouble into his life—because there's not a doubt in my mind that I'm the reason why it's here.

"Did you get him?" he asks, pocketing the phone and raising the weapon to his shoulder as he moves to step outside. I hold up my palm, signaling for him to stay where he is.

"I got him out of the tree," I say, not foolish enough to believe I managed to land a shot that I took blindly. But at least I managed to cost the shooter their advantage. "I'm not sure if he's alone, though."

Watching the last of my small cloud of smoke as it dissipates, I search for signs of a second sniper.

"So what now?"

"I don't know yet."

My teeth grit together, grinding as I weigh my options. The safest choice would be to stay where I am until backup arrives, but I'm not sure I can do that. I can't risk letting whoever this is get away, not when I have no idea who they are.

Before I can make a decision, the sound of tiny hooves trotting across the dirt reaches my ears. I spin toward the noise. Watch in horror as Stephano, the pygmy goat and most outgoing member of the rescues who live here at the sanctuary, heads straight toward where the shooter fell.

Panic rises in my throat, making my voice crack as I call his name. He glances briefly in my direction, then *baas* as he quickens his steps, choosing to ignore me. Cursing, I leave the shelter of the truck and chase after him.

It's stupid. It's reckless. But I have to do it. I'll never forgive myself if anything happens to him—to any of the animals here. It's my job to keep them safe and I dropped the ball. I should have expected something like this.

A pang of guilt lances through me as Jake calls my name. It grows as the heavy thud of his boots strike against the earth, racing behind me. It's almost enough to make me stop. Instead, I push an extra boost of speed into my legs. I need to make sure that I'm the closer target, that the gunman's decision is an easy one if he's lying in wait.

Catching up with Stephano as he reaches the tree line, I scoop him up into my arms. Hold his squirming body tight against mine as I spin, half expecting a spray of bullets to hit my back.

It doesn't happen, but that doesn't mean it's not coming. Because I've made some very powerful enemies lately. People like that don't just drop a grudge—they try to annihilate the source of it. Which means that since they failed this time, it isn't over.

CHAPTER 2

The lump in my throat grows as I watch the black bag on the stretcher get loaded into the medical examiner's transport van. I didn't kill the man it contains. None of my bullets pierced his flesh. Judging by the angle his head had been at when I'd crept forward with Stephano in my arms and taken a look at him, he broke his neck in the fall.

But that doesn't make the bitter taste coating my tongue any easier to swallow.

Maybe I should have waited. Not taken the shot. If I had, would the man still be alive? I'll never know the answer. What I do know is that as long as he was in the tree, I was safe. It would have been impossible for him to hit me where I was hiding behind the truck.

It's possible he would have died in a shootout with the Feds when they arrived with their lights flashing and their sirens blaring to take him into custody. But if he hadn't, if he had survived, would he have talked?

Could I have gotten the answers to some of the

questions twisting and turning through my mind with the force of an F5 tornado? More importantly, could I have had the blood of one less of my fellow humans on my hands? One less face to haunt my dreams when I close my eyes at night?

I'll never know now, and it's all my fault. I release a heavy sigh, aware that I need to stop thinking like this. It's accomplishing nothing.

Besides, it's not like I don't have an idea who's behind what happened. The first preliminary hearing is tomorrow. I'll be a key witness in the trial. Even without my testimony, the prosecutor has a strong case. But with it?

Well, chances are that this day would have been much less eventful if at least one person didn't think that silencing me would make a difference. But the people who murdered my parents had to have anticipated that it wouldn't be easy. I'm not the type of woman willing to just lie down and die.

I faced nearly insurmountable odds when I took them down, facing them on my own, and still I prevailed. Not to mention that I've been an FBI agent for the last fifteen years. True, most of that time was spent behind a desk instead of out in the field. And I'm technically on medical leave at the moment—again. Still, I've been assured that the Bureau still considers me a valuable asset.

I'd assumed that was why I haven't been pushed to retire yet, considering that I turned down the offer made by the Miami field office to join their ranks. Though I haven't had the time to plan my next steps with everything that's happened since I returned home to the Everglades, I've made my intentions to stay here clear. I figured they were hoping that their patience would pay off.

Now, for the first time, I can't help wondering about the agency's motives for keeping me on. It's not just that the jury might be slightly more swayed by my testimony if I'm a current and not former agent. If today's attempt on my life had been successful, it would have been considered a federal crime.

And given how dangerous the murderers who are going to trial are, I can't help suspecting that someone out there in our judicial system would prefer that. To be able to take charge and have the ball in their court, even if the expense was my life.

Spotting Agent Gellar approaching, I do my best to keep my expression emotionless, to not betray the fear that's slowly replacing the adrenaline in my veins. Though my experience with the agents at the Miami field office hasn't been the best, she hasn't given me a reason to distrust her. Yet.

"We're wrapping it up now. Should be out of your hair soon. How are you holding up?" she asks, giving me a sympathetic smile.

"Just fine."

"Did you get a look at the perp?"

"Yes."

"I don't suppose you recognized him?" She releases a disappointed sigh as I shake my head. "He didn't have any identification on him. We found a car abandoned about a mile down the road. Stolen, of course. We're running his prints now, but…"

She doesn't finish the statement. She doesn't have to. Knowing what we do, I'm sure none of us are holding our breath that the dead man's fingerprints will hold the key to his identity. These people have proven their ability to access the system and alter records like that before.

Records that only members of law enforcement have access to.

"Still, I think it's safe to assume that he has ties to Bianchi," she says.

Tony Bianchi is one of the people whose trial I'm responsible for. I'm the one who found the evidence linking him to my parents' murders. The one who got a recording of his accomplice discussing their roles in the crime. The one who's planning on testifying against them all.

But being a seasoned killer isn't what makes the man so dangerous. It's the breadth of his reach into the dark corners of the shadowy underworld. A reach that apparently still exists, despite being in prison awaiting trial.

Money will do that, I suppose. And if there's one thing the drug kingpin has, it's money.

"Janine's hearing is tomorrow, isn't it?" Agent Gellar asks, even though I suspect she already knows.

"Yes."

She looks toward the barn, where Jake's in silhouette as he finishes feeding and watering the animals for the night.

"Has that caused any… complications?"

Removing the fingertip that's somehow found its way between my teeth from my mouth I say, "No."

"Really? I find that hard to believe."

I give her a sharp look.

"Listen, I'm not trying to pry. But you have to admit, it's unorthodox. Testifying against your boyfriend's mother at her murder trial."

Swallowing down what feels like a burning lump of charcoal, I clench my jaw, refusing to react. Janine Walker had been my mom's best friend. And Jake had been mine. He'd been a part of my life from the day I drew my first breath, and if I get my way, he'll be a part of it until the day I draw my last.

But decades passed where we weren't in touch. After my parents died and Jake's mom abandoned him our lives took separate paths. It's been less than six months since we found our way back to each other. I don't intend to lose him again.

And I won't, I assure myself.

"Jake and I have spoken about it," I say in a low voice as he approaches. "He supports what I'm doing. He has no allegiance to his mother."

It might seem cold, but Jake has his reasons. Because after Janine Walker helped kill my parents, she'd left Jake with his abusive father. Even when she returned over thirty years later, it wasn't to reunite with him. It was to find the evidence she'd hidden at my grandfather's house so she could blackmail Bianchi after they'd fallen out.

But things didn't quite go according to her plan. Though she'd known that my grandfather had recently died, she hadn't known that I'd be at the sanctuary. And despite having had her fingerprints swapped in the system with another woman's, I figured out who she was—and what she'd done.

Agent Gellar gives me a tight-lipped smile that suggests she doesn't believe me. "Well, anyway, I wanted to offer to post a couple agents here overnight. I doubt they'd be foolish enough to try again so soon, but—"

"That won't be necessary," I say, ignoring the look Jake gives me as he joins us and hears what's being said.

As much as I'd love to give him the peace of mind that a federal security detail might provide him, I can't.

And I refuse to feel bad about it.

I don't know how many cops—or agents—Bianchi has on his payroll, but it's clear that he has at least one person on the inside. Considering that I don't have any idea who that might be, it's too big a risk. There's no way I could trust the people assigned to protect me.

I'd have to constantly look over my shoulder inside my own home as well as out, and the truth is, I'm exhausted. I need someplace—some time, as fleeting as those moments might be—to let my guard down enough to just breathe. Inviting a skilled enemy into my domain is the last thing I want to deal with.

"Why bother? Girl's got more lives than a dang cat."

Correction. Having to watch my back against an armed and trained federal agent with the possible intent to kill me is the second to last thing. Speaking to the man whose voice just made my teeth grit together hard enough to chip a molar is the first.

"You don't have to sound so disappointed by that," Jake says, slinging an arm around me as I turn to face Sheriff Kingston.

The man scowls. "And where were you when all this was happening?"

Swallowing down a splash of bile at the memory, I point toward the chunk of wood missing from the doorframe. "Here getting shot at, same as me."

But I don't think he gets the chance to hear what I've said, because Agent Gellar's response is louder and holds more menace.

"The real question is, where were you, Sheriff?"

He turns his glare to her. "Doing my job. Which, believe it or not, includes more than being a full-time babysitter for this one."

My mouth drops open. The only time the man could

be accused of keeping an eye on me is when I tried breaking up with his son back when we were in high school, and then it was only to make sure his threats had done their job and I stayed in the relationship until his son was through with me. Jake must notice my hands curling into fists because he tightens his arm around me.

"That might be so," Agent Gellar says, "but are we really supposed to believe that there were so many calls in your tiny town that you couldn't dispatch a single officer for"—she makes a show of checking her watch—"over two hours?"

Kingston shrugs, not even having the good grace to look ashamed.

"Are we done here?" I ask, having neither the energy nor the patience to prolong my suffering a moment longer than I have to.

"We are." Agent Gellar gives me a curt nod.

Trusting me to behave myself for the ten seconds it will take us to get inside, Jake releases his hold on me and opens the door.

"Goodnight, Agent Knox," Agent Gellar says as I'm stepping over the threshold. "And, Cassidy? Good luck."

I wave over my shoulder, not trusting my expression right now—or my voice. Because the way she said those parting words? It suggests that I'm going to need them. And honestly, I'm afraid she might be right.

CHAPTER 3

My hands shake. My chest is tight. And as I turn the deadbolt, I startle at the click because there's something almost ominous about the sound.

But at the same time, there's no denying the relief I feel at finally finding myself behind a locked door.

Out there, I have to be strong. Brave. Swallow my fear.

In here? I can crumble.

"Cassie." Jake's voice breaks over my name.

Turning to face him, I practically throw myself into his embrace. Bury my face in his chest as his arms tighten around me. Squeeze my eyes shut against the invading tears as he rests his chin against my head.

He holds me silently while my pulse slows. As my breath comes easier. Until the tension that had turned my muscles into stone eases.

"Cassie," he says again, whispering this time. "That was too close."

I nod against him, swallowing hard.

"I can't lose you."

"You won't."

"Maybe… maybe you should reconsider testifying."

I lean back until I can see his face, but he won't meet my eyes.

"You know I can't do that."

"But you could. They have Bianchi's fingerprints on the murder weapon. Pictures of the crime. My mom's confession. The prosecutor can get a conviction without you taking the stand."

"Exactly."

"Then why do it? I understand getting justice for your parents, but it's not worth the risk."

"I agree."

"You do?"

"Of course I do. Do you think I like being shot at?" I ask hoarsely, almost choking on the lump in my throat.

"Then should I call the DA? Tell him you've changed your mind?"

"No."

"Are you serious?"

"Completely. Jake—"

Releasing me, he crosses his arms. Shakes his head, jaw tense, nostrils flaring as he glares a hole into the wall. A spark of outrage lights inside my belly. Does he think I'm being difficult on purpose? That I somehow enjoy this?

"Don't you think that if there was something I could do to make this all go away that I would?" My voice rises as I step away, beyond his reach. Shooting a glance toward the door, afraid of being overheard, I force myself to take a breath and speak calmer. "It's too late for that."

I rub my temples, trying to ease the throbbing that's taken root. "You're not seeing the big picture. They know I don't need to testify to seal their convictions. They don't care. That's not what this is about."

"Then what is it about? Tell me, Cassie. I'm trying to understand."

Turning my back, I take a moment to compose myself so I'm not screaming when I say, "Revenge."

He curses. The couch creaks as he takes a seat. Risking a peek behind me, I find him cradling his head in his hands, fingers threaded through his dark hair.

"Let's leave," he says, without looking up.

"We can't do that."

"But we could."

"The animals—"

"We could find a chunk of land somewhere, open a new sanctuary. Pay someone to take care of them until we get settled, then send for them."

"But this is home," I say quietly. Swallowing hard, I add, "And even if it wasn't, leaving might not solve anything. I don't want to have to look over my shoulder for the rest of my life, worrying about them finding us."

"Then what do you suggest? That I just stand by and wait until the inevitable day comes when someone makes the shot? When you're the target?" His face is red, eyes moist as he looks up at me. "I can't do that. I won't."

I hate seeing him like this. Hate feeling like it's my fault, when it's not. It isn't his, either. We were just children when this was all set in motion.

Crossing to him, I take a seat on the arm of the couch beside him. Try to muster a smile, though I fail, as I cup his face in my hands.

"I'm not asking you to."

Wrapping an arm around me, he scoops me from my perch onto his lap. As I settle against him, I do my best to forget about the danger and the chaos, trying to focus only on the here and now—the way my heart feels like it's turning cartwheels when he holds me, the faint scent of soap still clinging to his skin, how, even now, when it seems like danger is lurking around every corner, I long to lose myself in him.

"I'm going to think of something. Find a way to fix this. We're going to take our lives back," I say. "I promise."

I hope that it's true. But if it's not? Then I pray that I've at least found a way to keep him safe when it turns out I'm wrong.

CHAPTER 4

My heart pounds like a heavy metal drummer. My skin feels like it's shrunk, tightening uncomfortably over sinew and bones. The acrid taste of anxiety coats the back of my tongue, the icy fingers of fear wriggling like worms over the back of my neck.

I draw deep breaths, struggling to compose myself. I need to calm down. Relax. Nothing bad is going to happen, and even if it were, having a panic attack will accomplish nothing other than damaging my pride. I can do this. I know I can.

And yet, I pause on the threshold before stepping completely outside, my fingers holding onto the open door with an iron grip, as if it's tethering me to safety. Even though it's morning, it's so early that it's still dark out, long shadows holding court until the sun rises to chase them away. A thick blanket of fog hovers low over the ground.

Anything could be hiding behind that misty vapor. Anyone. It's not a comforting thought.

I peer around, searching the gloom for signs of life. Listen closely, though the silence is eerily complete. Wait for the telltale prickle of eyes on my skin. But there's nothing. Just me feeling like a chicken as I stand here, working up my nerve to enter my own yard.

"Everything okay?"

I gasp as I jump. Whirl to face Jake.

"Sorry, I didn't mean to scare you."

I try to return his apologetic smile as I struggle to catch my breath. Allow him to pull me to his chest, where I close my eyes, listening to the strong beat of his heart.

"Maybe you should stay home today. It's not like you have to be there. It's just a preliminary hearing."

"No, I want to go."

"Are you sure?" He leans back until he can see my face. "You could go back to bed? Get some more sleep?"

It's a polite way of saying he's noticed the dark circles that ring my eyes. After yesterday's excitement, I was awake most of the night. I've been awake most of every night lately, to be honest, unwilling to subject myself to the nightmares that plague me.

It was bad enough finding myself back in the damp, pitch-black basement where a serial killer held me, as I often did in my darker dreams. But now, other dangers lurk in the corners of my subconscious.

I can still feel the force of the gun blast. The hot spray of blood hit my cheek. The fingers wrapped around my neck, tightening until my throat felt on the verge of collapse. Until my life started to drain away.

The bruises from my latest encounter with trouble have just faded. But given what happened last night, I'm beginning to wonder if I'll ever be able to close my eyes again without fearing the memories that hide behind them.

"I'm fine," I insist.

"Are you sure?"

Nodding, I release Jake and move out of his embrace. The lift of my chin is fueled more by stubbornness than bravery as I take the plunge and stride outside.

Jake falls into step beside me, lacing his fingers through mine. Lifts my hand to his lips.

"Don't you need to get ready for work?" I ask.

"I'm going in late today."

"Why?"

"Because I'm coming with you this morning."

"You don't have to do that."

"I know. But what do you think I'd rather do? Sit in my office looking at contracts and briefs and court dockets? Or look at you?"

When I cut my eyes over to him, he winks.

"If you want me to stop being corny, you'll have to help me find something else to do." He pulls me to a stop just inside the barn and turns to face me. Backs me up until I'm pressed against one of the stalls. Drops his head until his mouth hovers just above mine. "I have a few ideas of my own I'd like to share with you."

I close my eyes as his lips lower. But they deviate before they touch mine, landing on my neck instead. His kisses send shivers through me as they whisper across my skin, moving lower. My breath quickens as his hands sneak under the hem of my shirt, palms hot against my lower back.

Arching against him, I thread my fingers through his hair. It feels like I'm melting as the tension that's been holding my body rigid eases. The whirlwind of dark thoughts that have been swirling around inside my head fall still, silenced by the heat spreading through me. The desire.

Just as I'm about to suggest we go back inside, a thud hits one of the stall doors. I crack an eye open, groaning as Stephano frolics over. Taking the sound I made as a moan, Jake presses harder against me. Then he jerks, surprised, as tiny hooves pound against him.

"Not now, buddy," Jake tries, even though the goat has never been known to take no for an answer before.

Baa.

"Go play."

Baaaaa. I can't help snickering as Stephano sticks his tongue out, waggling it through the air. This time, Jake's the one who groans.

"Maybe if I feed him first," he offers.

A heavy striped head swings over the door beside us at the mention of feed. Daisy stretches her neck, her upper lip curling as the zebra tries to reach my hair. There's a flutter as Rocky appears, then an ear-splitting crow as the rooster wakes the rest of the world.

Soon, we're surrounded by the sounds of the animals as they stir from their slumber. Jake gives me a look so hopeless that I can't help but laugh.

"But—" he says, cut off as Stephano headbutts his knee.

"Later," I promise.

"How much later?"

"Tonight."

Jake sighs with disappointment. I press a kiss against his stubbled jaw, then slip from his embrace. Daisy nickers, waving her head through the air, urging me to bring her breakfast. Chip and Bagel, the pigs, oink from behind their door, not wanting to risk being forgotten at mealtime.

There's a lightness to my step as I hurry to the tack room to grab everyone's food while Jake gets to work freshening their waters. Would I rather be doing what I was five minutes ago than scooping grain? Definitely.

But I can't deny that I feel better than I had earlier. My mind is clearer, my confidence found. I plan to use the thoughts of what I have to look forward to later to help me get through the day, and let's face it—I need all the help I can get. Because there's a target on my back, and if the right person gets the chance, they're going to hit it.

CHAPTER 5

If looks could kill, I'd be a dead woman right now.

Fortunately, they can't. And people have tried using far deadlier methods against me before and failed. Still, I can't deny that it hurts. I'm sure plenty of mothers hate their son's girlfriend, but most of them probably wouldn't actually commit murder if given the chance.

Yet as Janine Walker glares at me from the seat beside her defense attorney, there's no denying what I see in her eyes. Hatred. Blood lust. Disgust. I'm sure the woman would have my head impaled on a stake if she could.

Rubbing my sweaty palms across the thighs of my slacks, I fight the urge to shift in my seat. Refuse to be the one to look away first. I know how any sign of weakness whets a predator's appetite. I refuse to be seen as prey.

Perhaps sensing my discomfort, Jake wraps an arm around my shoulders. He scoots closer, until I'm tucked against him. Plants a kiss against the side of my head.

Janine ends our staring contest, her gaze softening as it shifts to her son. Within seconds, it's hardened again, her entire expression turning to stone as her eyes flit between me and Jake. It's only then that I realize what he's doing—making it clear who he's chosen. And momma ain't happy about it.

If Jake notices her intense glare, he doesn't let on. He doesn't acknowledge her at all. Instead, he looks straight ahead, listening to the judge as he opens the preliminary hearing.

To the casual observer, the man next to me would appear completely calm and relaxed, but I know better. The telltale signs of his distress are there, in the way his forefinger rubs against the cuticle on his thumb. The shallowness of his breathing. How tight he's holding me.

He makes a small *hmm* noise. I glance up to find the stoic expression he's been wearing replaced by a frown. It grows as I watch. My muscles tense, I follow his gaze to the bench, where Janine's defense attorney is speaking to the judge in a voice too low for the rest of the courtroom to hear.

The judge's eyebrows rise. He adjusts his glasses. Finally, he nods.

Clearing his throat, he says, "Due to an unexpected development, I'm accepting the defense's motion to delay proceedings. We'll postpone until next Monday."

I look at Jake, not understanding what's just happened.

"Is that normal?" I whisper.

"No."

"Should we be worried?"

"I'm not sure."

Janine stands, casting a final poisonous scowl at me as she's led away by the bailiff. Beside me, Jake rises to his feet.

"Come on," he says, holding his hand out for mine. "Let's see if we can find out what's going on."

We hurry after the prosecutor as he leaves the courtroom.

"Hey, Dennis," Jake calls.

The man stops and turns around. His polite smile turns genuine when he sees us.

"Well look what the cat dragged in. Jake Walker. How are things over at Myers and Kleinman? The dark side been keeping you busy?"

"You know evil—it never rests."

I force a smile onto my face as the men share a laugh. I wasn't aware that Jake knew the DA. Given that they're both big lawyers in a small pond, I suppose I shouldn't be surprised. What does surprise me, though, is that Jake never mentioned it.

Dennis Farber's attention shifts to me. "And, Agent Knox. It's nice to see you. I appreciate you coming out today to show your support. You two know each other?"

"We're together," Jake says.

"I wasn't aware. How long have—"

"Any idea what just happened in there?" Jake interrupts, too impatient to keep engaging in small talk.

"You mean the Walker—" The man's expression clouds over with confusion. His brows knit together. "Wait." His eyes dart between me and Jake. "Are you related to the defendant?"

"She's my mother," Jake admits in a tight voice.

The man clears his throat. Lasers a steely look at me as he says, "And you're my star witness. Is this going to be an issue?"

"Only if you let it be," Jake answers rather brusquely. "We're all on the same page here, Dennis. My mother is a dangerous person. She needs to spend the rest of her life in prison."

"Actually, we've decided to go for the death penalty."

A muscle in Jake's jaw tics. "Since when?"

"We just made the decision this morning."

"Is that what the delay is about?"

"No. Your guess is as good as mine about that. It's probably a move made by Bianchi's defense team, but I wouldn't worry about it. They can't change the facts. We definitely have enough evidence to prove probable cause and go to trial."

If you believe what's been reported in the local papers, Tony Bianchi's lawyers have done their best to turn Janine into their sacrificial lamb. And given that he has a legal dream team that's somehow managed to delay his trial and all related proceedings until after hers is complete, and that she's being represented by a public defender, I'm willing to buy it. Still, I fail to see what they stand to gain by pulling a last-minute move like this.

The mystery behind the delay, all the unknowns, this entire conversation is making me anxious. Just the idea that the people who murdered my parents might somehow finagle their way out of paying for their crimes makes it feel like an invisible vise has clamped around my chest, tightening until I can barely breathe.

I need to get out of here before I do something stupid. Or worse, something to embarrass Jake. Blessedly, my cell rings, sparing my addled brain from having to think of an excuse. Catching Jake's eye, I hold up my phone and gesture that I'm going to step away before leaving the two men to their discussion.

"Hello?"

"Cassidy, it's Donna."

The last time the owner of the small feed store in my tiny hometown of Gator Glade called me, I ended up with a giant rooster and an enraged cockfighter on my hands. Which means this will either be exactly what I need, or the last thing I need right now. Either way, I'm grateful for the diversion.

"Hey, what's up?"

"I just had someone call to report an animal in need of rescue out on the Indigo Hammock trail. I was hoping maybe you'd be able to go check it out."

I open my mouth to respond, then clamp it shut so hard that my molars clip the edge of my tongue. Indigo Hammock is miles off the beaten path. Even farther from help, should someone out there need it. My heart races as the memory of the sniper's red dot on my T-shirt yesterday fills my mind. I quickly push it away.

Taking a deep breath, I cup my free hand over the pulse throbbing in my neck as I say, "Sure. What am I looking for?"

"She said it was a raccoon. Poor thing has its head stuck in something metal. About two and a half, maybe three miles in."

Three miles. Most hikers don't make it that far into the trails around here in the heat, not unless they're local, which I'm sure Donna would have mentioned if this woman was. My throat tightens, making it difficult to swallow. What if it's a trap? Then again, what if it's not?

Sweat pricks at my skin as I argue with myself. I refuse to live in fear. Whoever's after me would know I have more sense than to hike out into the middle of the woods alone—even if I actually don't.

Because I have to live my life normally. I can't let them take that from me. And there's no way I can risk the chance that an animal in need goes unattended. Even if it is a really stupid decision… one that I shouldn't even consider.

What would my grandfather do?

Easy. Butch would hike out and do his best to find the raccoon. Plus, chances are that the hiker estimated the distance wrong. One mile can feel like five when you practically have to swim through the humidity.

"Did she sound sure of the distance?"

"Er… no. But she said she'd been walking at a steady pace for a little over an hour when she saw it. And that she found some sticks, laid them in the middle of the path in the shape of an arrow pointing toward where it was."

I stifle a groan. Depending on how fast she was going, the woman could have made it even farther than she'd guessed in that time.

That's a long way to hike on the off chance that the animal is still able to be spotted from the trail. Even longer if I do find it and discover that I need to carry it out for medical attention. But I won't be able to sleep tonight, thinking about it out there in need of help, if I don't at least try to find it. And it will definitely be a distraction.

Casting a glance at Jake, I find him still in discussion with DA Farber. Given what happened last night, he won't be happy about me heading that far into the woods alone.

"Sounds easy enough," I lie. "I'll swing by the house and grab some gear, then set out."

"Great. Let me know how it goes."

Ending the call, I return to Jake's side just as his conversation with the DA is wrapping up.

"I'll give you a buzz, let you know what I find out," Dennis says, holding up a rectangle of paper I recognize as one of Jake's business cards.

"I appreciate it."

"And, Agent Knox, I'll let you know as soon as we have a court date and I have an idea of when you'll be needed for your testimony."

"Thank you."

A round of handshakes later, Jake wraps an arm around me as we watch the district attorney go.

"Everything all right?" I ask.

"Yeah. How about with you?"

"Just something that Donna needs some help with."

"You've got to go, then?"

"Yeah, I probably should."

"I'll walk you to your car."

My eyebrows shoot up my forehead. That was easier than I thought it would be. I hurry to bring my expression back to neutral, but I can't deny the rush of both surprise and relief that he isn't asking about where I'm going and what I'll be doing after what happened yesterday.

Not to mention it's an odd thing to say, considering we're parked next to each other. I keep the thought to myself as we cross the parking lot, figuring his mom's case has him distracted. Do my best to make my smile genuine as I turn to face him. But the kiss he drops on my forehead leaves a lot to be desired.

He waits as I get settled behind the wheel, buckle my seat belt, and start the engine.

"Drive safe," he says, his eyes meeting mine only briefly before he presses my door closed.

Something's wrong. A lot of things are actually, but this something is different. Unexpected. And though I try to tell myself I'm imagining things as I linger at the stop sign watching Jake walk back into the courthouse, I'm sure that I'm not.

CHAPTER 6

I wipe at the sweat dripping into my eyes. Take deep breaths, trying to ease the pounding of my heart. Do my best to maintain a positive inner monologue, trying to convince myself I'll be okay. But I'm losing the battle. I don't have much fight left in me.

It's been a long time since I've done this. Too long. It isn't only that I'm ill-prepared, although there's no denying that's true. It isn't even the heat, which feels like it's boiling my brain and sucking my will to survive out through my dehydrating pores. It's that I'm starting to think this is pointless.

According to my GPS, I've gone just over three miles, and so far, other than a few small birds darting through the underbrush and one very scruffy-looking squirrel, I haven't seen anything. Not the raccoon, not the arrow made of branches, not even the other two hikers who signed the trail log ahead of me and should still be out here.

Slipping my hands under the straps of my pack, I

hoist it higher on my back. My long-sleeved sun shirt beneath is drenched. My shoulders beg for a break, unaccustomed to the weight of the gear I carry. And my nerves… well, let's just say they've had better days.

I've had nothing to do but think for the last hour and the conclusion I've reached is that coming out here by myself was a really stupid idea. I run the conversation I had with Donna through my mind for the dozenth time.

The woman who spotted the raccoon in need of help called the report in. As far as I know, she didn't give her name. No one saw her face. The time marked by the two hikers who checked in before me indicates that they started their hike after the woman made the call, but their names were the only ones entered this morning, which means she didn't even sign the trail log.

In fact, so far there's been nothing to indicate there's any truth to her story. But why lie?

Despite the heat, a chill races through me, goosebumps rippling across my skin as I think of an answer. One I may have dismissed too easily. Because if you wanted to get someone to let their guard down, to lure them away from their home turf to a place where you could catch them off guard, bait them into a situation where they'd have a hard time escaping, what that woman did was an excellent way to go about it.

My pulse kicks into overdrive, the rush of blood leaving me lightheaded. I grab onto the nearest tree, waiting for the dizziness to pass. I'd been so focused on not giving in to fear that I completely ignored the fact that I *should* be afraid.

But are these people that smart?

Calling the feed store instead of the sanctuary directly, knowing Donna would call me and I'd be the one to respond? Being vague about the distance, so I'd keep going until I'd made my way far beyond the reach of help? To a place where no one would even hear me scream?

A scraping noise sounds behind me, so foreign to the sounds of the woods that the world around me falls silent. I gasp so hard I practically choke. Draw my pistol from its holster as I twist around. Pressing my spine hard against the tree I'd been leaning against, I search the shadows for the source, eyes straining wide with the effort.

I hear the clatter again, though I don't see any movement. My heart kicks against the walls of my chest, berating me for being such a fool. I didn't tell Jake where I was going specifically because I knew coming out here by myself with everything that was going on was a dumb idea. Now, if I don't make it home tonight, he won't even know where to look.

Not that there would be much hope of my body being discovered way out here. There are too many places to dispose of it, too many creatures to eagerly feed on my remains.

Sharp fingernails of panic claw at me. I try to draw deep, calming breaths, but my lungs fail to fully inflate. The panic attacks that plagued me after I escaped a serial killer's basement, the ones I thought I had overcome, have returned. Bark scrapes painfully against my back as I slide to the ground.

I promise myself I won't go down easily, not without putting up a heck of a fight, but even my hands fail me, shaking too hard to rack the slide as I try to chamber a round. But as movement shakes the underbrush to my right, the surge of adrenaline helps me get the job done.

"FBI." My voice sounds weak, shaky. Conjuring my

former self, I bark, "Come out slowly with your hands up. Do it now!"

A palmetto rustles, then another, the motion moving away from me. There's no way I want to be stuck out here, looking over my shoulder for the entire three-plus miles back to the trailhead.

"Stop or I'll shoot."

Bracing myself with my free hand, I push to my feet. The change in viewpoint reveals the last thing I expected. Quickly, I launch into pursuit.

Though it doesn't take me long to catch up, I have to be careful. This next part is tricky.

I re-holster my firearm as I shadow my quarry. Slip off my pack and pull it on across the front of my chest, then unzip the pouch. Grab out the long, thick leather gloves I packed right at the top.

The instant I touch the raccoon's back, it releases a startled screech. It reverses frantically, trying to get away, but the metal lodged over its head keeps that from happening. It paws at the trap, at my hands, at everything, trying to get free, but it can't.

Though not a baby, it's young, still a kit. It squeaks and cries instead of growling and hissing. And I can tell, as it wraps one of its silky little hands around my fingers, that it's weak. There's no telling how long its head has been stuck like this.

I gently pinch the loose skin between its shoulder blades. Instead of springing back when I release it, the flesh remains tented. This creature is dehydrated. And while that could happen quite quickly in the South Florida heat, that doesn't make it any less dangerous.

Murmuring softly, I crouch over the raccoon, holding it in place with my legs as I riffle through my bag. Withdraw a pair of small shears. Push down on its neck until I get enough slack to slip one blade inside the trap. And then I get to work.

Progress is slow. Between the raccoon's squirming and not having the best tool for the job, it's hard going. But finally, keeping a finger over the ragged metal edge, I'm able to work the trap over the animal's head.

And it is a trap, one of the old metal types we used to catch bait in when I was little. Strange to find it so far out here, in the middle of nowhere. But I don't get much time to think about it. Because though I'd expected the raccoon to scamper off once free, it doesn't. It remains where it is with its eyes shut, panting.

Concerned, I grab a bowl from my bag and fill it with water. The raccoon curls its tiny hands around the rim, drinking greedily. Still it keeps its eyes closed.

I lean forward for a closer look. Sigh heavily and unstrap the collapsible carrier from the bottom of my pack. Though I've been intending to re-open the medical care part of the sanctuary, I don't have the facilities completely ready yet.

But it seems I'm out of time. I just got my first patient.

I wait until my new ward has finished drinking, then make the kit as comfortable as I can in the carrier. Though I consider wearing the gloves in case I need to reach the animal quickly, I ultimately decide to return them to my bag.

Because even though the call that brought me out here was legitimate, that doesn't mean I'm safe. I have a long—and with the extra weight I'm going to be carrying, no doubt arduous—hike back to the trailhead. And though I was never a Girl Scout, that doesn't mean I don't believe in their motto: *Be Prepared.* Which means keeping my trigger finger at the ready.

CHAPTER 7

My limbs are weak. My muscles won't stop trembling. And my pride is seriously damaged.

Though it took me only an hour to hike in to where I found the raccoon, the hike out took almost two. I had to stop—frequently—to slip the gloves back on to give the kit water. But more than that, to give my weary arms a rest.

An extra ten pounds might not seem like much, but when you're carrying it in front of you, and trying to do it gently, for miles, it adds up. By the time I reach the trailhead, my arms are shot.

I set the carrier on the ground beside the mailbox where the trail log is kept, my cramped hand barely managing to grab the pen inside and illegibly scrawl the time I'm leaving to sign out. Before I close the door on the notebook, I shake my head in admiration at Amelia Owens and Danielle Fuller, the two hikers who checked in before me and are still out on the trail in this heat.

Only, as I pick the raccoon back up and reach the

small dirt parking lot, I realize that my car is the only one there. The same was true when I arrived. I guess they must have forgotten to sign out, which means that I was on the trail alone the whole time. The thought further unsettles my already upset stomach, but it's too late to worry about my foolishness now.

Though I'm anxious to get going, I blast the air conditioner for several minutes, cooling the sweltering interior of the vehicle before I place the carrier in the back seat, strapping it in place with the seat belt. I can't wait to get home, drink a gallon of water, and try to work the knots out of my shoulders under the spray of a steaming hot shower. Unfortunately, I have to make a stop first.

By the time I turn off the Tamiami onto the narrow road leading into Gator Glade, I'm no less exhausted, but at least my clothes have almost dried, although they're uncomfortably stiff with sweat. But it was all worth it—the heat, the strain, the fatigue. Because as I pull into the parking lot of the small pharmacy in town, the raccoon is chittering away. It's music to my ears.

I'm glad the little guy is feeling better, especially considering that the vet finally returned my text, responding that he wouldn't be able to stop by until tomorrow morning. Until then, I'll do my best to keep the sanctuary's newest rescue as happy and comfortable as I can.

Which is why I'm here. Though I suspect the kit's eye infection will require antibiotics to clear up, the least I can do is get some saline to flush them. With an ounce of luck, I'll be able to remove enough of the crust and goo for them to open. Leaving the car running with the AC on, I lock the doors and go inside.

Instantly I find myself overcome by the sensation

that I've been transported back into the past, and not just because I haven't been in here since I was a teenager. It doesn't appear like much, if anything, has changed.

To my left is the same ancient gumball machine that I used to beg dimes off my grandfather for. The poster of a man in a yellow coat and brown slacks eating ice cream still hangs behind the ice chest beside the front counter. Even the smell, a curious mix of camphor and bubble gum that calls to mind the taste of the medication that made getting an ear infection seem like a treat as a child, is the same.

I make my way slowly down the aisles, scanning the shelves for what I need. Smile as I spot a little girl standing in line with her mother near the pharmacist's counter at the back, watching me. She ducks her head behind her mother's leg to hide, but just before I turn the next corner, she looks at me again and offers a shy wave.

Waving back, I make eye contact with her mom. The woman looks familiar. Many of these people do. And the man behind the counter? To my surprise, it's Phil Johnson. The pharmacist must be over seventy now. I'm surprised he hasn't retired.

But that's the way it is here in Gator Glade. It's a small town. The kind that doesn't have enough to offer to bring a new generation of fresh blood in. Chances are, when Mr. Johnson finally decides to stop working, the pharmacy will close. I feel a pang of sadness at the thought.

"Oof."

I'm knocked backward as a man rounds the corner, banging into me.

"Sorry," I say, though the incident wasn't my fault.

I watch his back as he continues on without acknowledging me.

"Rude," I mutter to myself, then forget my indignation as I finally spot the saline solution, down on the very bottom shelf. I wince, my stiff muscles straining as I reach for it. Straighten up, still empty-handed, as a collective gasp rises from the back of the store.

A loud voice rolls over the aisles like thunder. A teenager runs by me, racing out the front door. Something in my gut tells me I should follow.

But do I? No. Though I never considered myself as lacking common sense, today's obviously an exception. I head toward the trouble, instead.

Creeping to the end of the aisle, I peer around the corner. My eyes are immediately drawn to the little girl I'd seen earlier. Once again, she has her head hidden behind her mother's leg. This time, she has a reason.

I pull out my phone, intending to alert 911 before I take any action, but there's no time. A cry of fear comes from the small crowd cowering in front of the pharmacy counter as the man trespassing behind it—the same one who knocked into me only moments ago—racks the slide on the firearm he holds before shoving it against Mr. Johnson's temple.

"Hurry up, old man."

A surge of anger ignites beneath my skin. Mr. Johnson's hands shake as he pulls boxes from a shelf, transferring them to the bag the man holds. As the man jabs the gun harder into the pharmacist's head, one of the packages misses its intended destination and falls to the floor.

My gut knots as I see that it's a generic allergy medication. One that contains pseudoephedrine, an ingredient used to make methamphetamine. I swallow hard as I step out from the aisle, revealing myself.

If the man holding the gun is tweaking right now,

coming down off his last high, that makes him incredibly dangerous. Not just impatient, but irrational, violent, possibly even paranoid.

He curses, gesturing for Mr. Johnson to pick up the dropped box. The elderly man trembles as he spreads his legs, grabbing onto the shelf for balance as he tries to reach the floor.

"Hurry up, hurry up."

"Here."

I hold my hands up as I approach, trying to signal that I mean no harm. But it's a lie. I totally do.

There are seven rounds in the small pistol concealed beneath my shirt, and I'll gladly put every single one of them into this guy's skull if it means keeping any of the innocent people here from being hurt.

"Let me," I say, slowly approaching the open counter gate.

The man eyes me warily as I step through the gap. "Who are you?"

"My name's Cassidy," I say calmly. "I want to help."

"No." The way the man shakes his head, too fast and erratically, one shoulder twitching with the motion, suggests that he is, indeed, tweaking right now. "Get over there with the rest of them. I want him to do it."

Mr. Johnson's eyes flash with fear, but as they meet mine, I see something else in them, too. Recognition.

"I'm not sure that he can," I explain. "It can be hard for an older person to get something off the floor. Please, let me help."

The entire time I talk, I continue inching forward. The man shifts the gun's aim from Mr. Johnson to me as I come to a stop several feet away. Slowly, hands still held out, I start squatting.

"I said no!"

Given how hard the strike hits my cheekbone, I'd be willing to bet it was the firearm and not the man's fist that made contact. Neither changes the fact that I've been knocked off my feet, flying back to the other side of the counter, bottles of alcohol and hydrogen peroxide scattering across the floor as I hit the endcap where they were displayed.

Fireworks explode inside my head. My face throbs. And my anger turns to rage.

I take a deep breath as I lie on my side on the floor. Place one hand in front of me, ready to push myself up, the other behind me like I'm going to grab the shelf against my back for support. But I tell myself to wait.

The man curses again. The gun wavers through the air, bouncing from me, to the terrified shoppers, to Mr. Johnson, then finally toward the ceiling as he clutches at his hair with both hands. I may not get a better opportunity than right now.

In an instant, I've drawn my weapon and pushed myself into a sitting position. Slapping my left hand over the fingers of my right, already curled around the grip of my gun, I aim the pistol at an invisible X I imagine on the center of the man's skull.

"Drop your weapon."

His eyes widen. I can see the gears turning inside his head. This isn't going to end well.

Slipping my finger inside the trigger guard, I give him one final chance. "Put it down now."

A high-pitched shriek sounds from my left. I glance toward it, trying to stay on top of the situation. Spot the little girl, now watching, her mouth open wide with fright though the rest of her cries are silent.

In an instant I return my gaze to the gunman. His top

half has already disappeared into the aisle I vacated only minutes ago as he leaps toward escape. And though I yearn to pull the trigger, to sink a chunk of metal into his hindquarters to impede his progress, I don't.

It's too late. His steps are loud and heavy as he runs to the front of the store. Then he's gone.

I screwed up. I just let a very dangerous man get away. Which means the already hazardous world is that much more unsafe. And if that man sees me again, and recognizes me, so am I.

CHAPTER 8

The muscles in my neck spasm, pulled impossibly tight. My nails dig deep into my palms. Though I long to open my mouth, to try and relieve some of the tension in my jaw, I don't dare. Because if I release my tongue from where it's clamped between my teeth, I'm definitely going to say something.

And it's not going to be nice.

I turn toward my car, overwhelmed with guilt that the poor raccoon is still trapped in the carrier in my back seat. Even with the air conditioner running, it can't be too comfortable in there. I need to hurry up and get it home.

Which is exactly what I told Sheriff Kingston almost an hour ago when he arrived. But instead of being one of the first that he interviewed, it appears he's saving me for one of the last.

I take deep breaths, telling myself that they're supposed to be calming, but they're not. I don't see how anything could be under the circumstances short of a coma, which is probably what it would take to block out the deep-seated anger stirred within me by my present company.

Anger that's been harboring inside me for over two decades now. Anger that begs to be unleashed. I clench my molars together a little harder and promise myself this will all be over soon.

"Where do you think you're going? Not trying to sneak off after creating such a huge mess, are you?"

I spin back around. Lock eyes with the man before me wishing, not for the first time, that I could tell him what I think of him. But I can't.

Although being exposed to Sheriff Kingston's delightful personality twice in less than twenty-four hours is a bitter pillow to try and swallow, here in the small town of Gator Glade, he's in charge. Since he could make my life even more difficult if he wanted to, which is the last thing I need, I'm forced to play nice.

"No," I say. "Like I told you earlier, I have a rescue in my car. I was just looking to see how many witnesses you had left to speak with."

"That's none of your concern. It's my job, not yours."

I force a smile.

"The last thing I need is for you to muddy up the waters before I get to the bottom of this."

Considering that the sheriff's investigative abilities are so poor I doubt he'd be able to find his own hand in a glove, I have zero hope that the man who robbed the pharmacy will ever be brought to justice.

"You're lucky that you're not facing charges."

My mouth drops open. "For what?"

"Reckless endangerment."

"Are you serious?"

"As a heart attack. I don't know what it was that you think you were doing back there, but you're lucky you didn't get any of those people hurt. You're not a cowboy. If you think I'm going to just stand by and let you turn my town into the wild west, you're mistaken. And another thing—"

"Cassidy, honey."

Mr. Johnson hobbles over. Gives me a wobbly smile as his gnarled fingers wrap around my arm.

"I wanted to make sure to catch you before you left. I can't thank you enough for coming to my rescue the way you did. It took a lot of courage, intervening like that. I don't think many people would have had the nerve. There was something crazed in that boy's eyes."

He shudders, then turns to Kingston.

"You should offer this young lady a job, Sheriff."

The sheriff and I exchange wary looks, both of us horrified by the thought of working together. Sensing the friction between us, the pharmacist's smile falters.

"You come see me before you leave, dear. I'll get you something for that bruise of yours."

"Thank you, Mr. Johnson. I appreciate the offer, but that isn't necessary. I need to hurry up and get home. I have an injured raccoon in my car that I need to get back to the sanctuary."

"Well, if it gives you any trouble, you come back and see me. I'll take good care of you."

He gives my arm a gentle squeeze before releasing me.

"We're all glad you came back home, honey. Butch would be so proud of you. There's no telling what would have happened if you hadn't been here."

I watch him shuffle off, feeling misty-eyed and choked with emotion.

"Don't you let what he said go to your head now. You got lucky back there."

"I know."

"You—" Kingston's head pulls back, his chin tucking into his neck. He blinks at me, obviously surprised that I agreed with him.

I take another one of those deep, not-so-calming breaths, and say, "Believe it or not, Lyle, I don't go looking for trouble."

"I don't know what you expect when you go waving your gun around like that."

Shaking my head, I sigh. "I didn't intend to get involved, but I couldn't stand by while Mr. Johnson got manhandled. I only drew my weapon after the man struck me and started aiming at customers. The threat escalated. I had no choice."

"Well, that may be true," he admits grudgingly. "But if you plan to stay in my town, I expect you to toe the line, you hear me? No more of these showoff stunts of yours. I don't want to see you again for a good long while."

"Believe me, I'm going to try my best to make that happen."

"Ugh. That already looks bad. Bet it's *not* going to be pretty in the morning."

Recognizing the voice, my shoulders rise beneath my ears. I close my eyes, praying that if I do, he'll disappear and I won't have to deal with him on top of everything else.

"You should really put some makeup on, try to cover that mess up."

No such luck.

"Whatcha doing here, son?"

My skin bristles as my high school boyfriend says,

"I heard that Cass here was involved in some trouble. Figured I'd pop over and see if it was true."

As I watch, Sheriff Kingston claps a heavy hand onto his son's back. Seeing them standing side by side, it's everything I can do not to launch an attack. A simple mistake I made when I was fifteen—dating the wrong boy—turned into a decision that would haunt me for years, until I managed to escape to college.

Even then, I let the fear of these men, the sheriff's power and by proxy, his son's, keep me away from my home for two decades. I missed so much because of them. Being a part of my grandfather's life. The sanctuary. Jake.

"How about you and me grab a few drinks, Cass? Let me get you feeling better?"

Kingston looks between me and his son. Matt, with his leering grin. Me, my simmering rage no doubt evident on my face to anyone not blinded by an enormously overinflated ego.

"That's never going to happen," I say.

"It could."

Some things never change. Matt still doesn't know how to take no for an answer.

"Trust me. It won't."

Kingston's jaw clenches so hard that I hear the joint pop. "Matt—"

Matt shoves a hand in his father's face, cutting him off with a blatant show of disrespect. Frankly, I'm amazed that the sheriff puts up with it. But that doesn't mean I have to.

"We're done here," I say to them both. Holding the sheriff's gaze, I say, "I'm going home."

"Why don't I join you?" Matt offers.

"You're not welcome on my property."

"What, is that some rule that Jake guy's trying to make for you?"

"No, it's a rule that *I'm* making for *you.* In front of the sheriff." Turning toward the man, I hold his gaze and say, "I've told him before, I'm telling you now. If he shows up again, I'll be pressing charges for trespassing."

Lyle returns my look for a long moment before giving a curt nod. On this, at least, we're on the same page. He doesn't want his son around me any more than I do. No matter what I've accomplished in my life, to him, I'll always be swamp scum.

"Noted."

I can't help smirking as I listen to them argue as I walk away. With any luck, that's one less problem to worry about. It's just too bad that there are so many other—deadlier—ones waiting.

CHAPTER 9

The noise of the deadbolt turning carries from the front of the house. My chest tightens. My muscles tense. My breathing shallows. The moment I've been dreading is here.

I continue to wash the dishes, pretending I'm unaware that I'm no longer alone. I knew I couldn't put this off indefinitely, but I'm not ready. I need more time.

As an arm slips around my waist, I close my eyes. Lean back, allowing my body to go slack. Savor these last few seconds of "before."

"Hey." Jake kisses my cheek, then rests his head against mine. "How was your day?"

"Eh. I've had better. How about yours?"

"Same."

"Why? What happened?" Concern has the water off, my hands empty, and me turned around all before I remember.

Jake's focus immediately zeros in on my bruised skin. His expression turns pained as he curses.

"I'm fine," I assure him. "It's nothing."

"It's not nothing." His eyes squeeze shut like he can't even stand to look at me. Pinching his temples, he draws a shaky sigh and says, "I knew it."

"You knew someone was going to rob the drugstore today? Next time, I wish you'd tell me."

"Wait." His hand drops, gaze meeting mine. "What?"

I nod.

"Which drugstore?"

"The one in Gator Glade."

"And your face just happened to get in the way of a fist?"

"That, or the butt of a gun. I really can't say for sure."

Jake curses again as he reaches for me. His thumb brushes lightly across the purple shiner that's already formed beneath my eye. "Are you sure you're okay?"

"Yes."

"You've got to stop doing this, Cassie."

A wave of heat ripples under my skin. I take a deep breath, trying to push it down, but I feel it gathering, rising, cresting, ready to unleash with the force of a tsunami. "Doing what?"

"Whatever you did that separated you from the people there who didn't get hurt."

"I didn't have a choice," I say tightly. "Some tweaker was knocking Mr. Johnson around."

His eyebrows crease together as he asks, "The same Mr. Johnson who was the pharmacist when we were kids?"

"Yes."

"What is he? Seventy-something? Eighty?"

I nod. "Do you understand now?"

The raised vein throbbing at Jake's temple slowly sinks back beneath his skin. "Yeah, but I still don't like it."

"Well, neither do I."

We stare at each other for a few moments in silence before he releases a heavy sigh and wraps his arms around me. I burrow against his chest. For the first time since we left the house this morning, the tension that's kept me in knots eases. Then, I remember what he said when he first saw me.

"What did you mean by 'you knew it?'"

"What?"

I push back until I can see his eyes. "When you saw my bruise, you said you knew it."

He releases me and turns away, crossing to the refrigerator. Says, "Just that something bad was going to happen. I've had a funny feeling all day."

I'm not sure it's the truth. If it is, it's not the full one. I wish I could see his face, but it's hidden behind the freezer door as he riffles around inside. "What do you have against frozen peas?"

"Peas are disgusting. They're an abomination against other vegetables."

"Agreed. But they're great for icing a shiner." Closing the door he gives me a smirk. "You'd think a girl like you would know that by now."

"Haha. Besides, I'd rather bruise than use ice. I hate the cold."

"Too bad." Grabbing a dishtowel from the counter, he wraps a handful of cubes inside it.

"You can keep that," I tell him.

"Nope. It will make you feel better, I promise. Now come here."

"Uh-uh."

I dart around the island to make my escape, but he's too fast. I laugh as he catches me, half carrying me to the table, where he points for me to take a seat. Grabbing him by the tie, I press my lips to his.

"Can't we do this instead?"

He gives me a grin, but it's a weak shadow of the one he usually wears. "Tell you what. Let's do this, fir—" The smile vanishes, replaced by a frown as he looks around. "What was that?"

"What was what?"

The kit chitters again from the crate in the corner, where it's woken up from its nap.

"That?"

I stand and point as I nonchalantly say, "You mean my new raccoon?"

Jake gives me a look as he crosses the room. Slowly, he sinks into a squat in front of the crate, where the kit has an arm stretched through the gate grid, reaching toward him.

My heart melts as I watch him offer the raccoon his finger. His thumb tenderly strokes the tiny hand that wraps around it.

"Has Craig been by yet?" he asks, referencing the vet.

"He can't make it until tomorrow. That's why I stopped at the drugstore. To get some saline to flush his eyes."

"He's not scared of us at all, is he?"

"Doesn't seem to be. That's why I have him in here with me. He kept crying when I left him alone."

"Was he a direct surrender?"

Sometimes, when people discover that they can't handle the wild animal they've tried to adopt, they'll surrender it to a rescue. In those cases, the animal has usually become habituated to being fed and will need to remain in captivity. Though that's not what happened here, given this guy's behavior, I predict the outcome will be the same.

"Nope. Had a bait trap stuck on his head."

Easing the abandoned towel filled with ice off the table, I set it quietly into the sink. Then, I return and take a seat.

"So, what do you think? Can I keep him?" I joke.

Jake smiles at the raccoon still holding his finger. "I think you're going to have to. Which means he's going to need a name. Any ideas?"

"I think we should wait until the vet examination for that."

"You're worried he might—" He darts a glance between me and the kit, not wanting to say anything negative about survival out loud.

"Oh, no. I think the raccoon will be fine."

"Then why?"

"Because judging by the way it's making eyes at you, I'm starting to suspect that he might be a she."

I try not to feel jealous at the way Jake's smile grows. At the look he's giving the animal before him. But mostly, I'm relieved that he's preoccupied.

Jake hasn't asked me where I found the raccoon yet. And I really hope the question's not in our future. I'm not going to lie to him, but I'm also not going to volunteer the information.

Because I saw his expression when he first spotted my bruised face. There was concern, yes, but beneath that was something else—anger. And if he was mad about me intervening at the drugstore, he'll be absolutely enraged if he finds out I spent hours alone in the woods without even telling him where I was.

I might be reckless, but I'm not stupid. I may act like it sometimes, but I'm not. I know there's a giant bullseye on me right now. I know I need to do something about it before someone hits their mark. But right now, I don't have a clue what that something is, which means my only recourse is to be careful. And so far, I'm doing a horrible job of that.

CHAPTER 10

I wake with a gasp. Lie still in the dark as I catch my breath, straining to hear any sounds in the house. But there's nothing. Not the creak of a door, the shuffle of a foot, not even the sound of Jake sleeping next to me.

My hand inches over the side of the mattress, to the grip of the pistol tucked beneath. I pull it out slowly, then sit up. Grab my phone from the nightstand and turn the screen on, using it to light the room. Just as I thought, I'm alone.

Slipping from the bed, I pull on my bathrobe, knotting the belt tight around my waist. Drop my cell in the pocket. Shove my feet into a pair of tennis shoes. Then, with gun in hand, I cross the room and ease the door open.

I creep down the hallway toward the room I'd spent hours cleaning and organizing earlier—the spare bedroom Butch used to refer to as the medical ward. Though somewhere along the way it had found a new use as a storage space in the years since he' d stopped taking injury cases, it's now back to serving its original purpose.

As I step inside, my eyes land on its newest patient. The kit lies curled in a corner of a cage that stretches almost the entire width of the room. As the only resident, there was no need to put the raccoon in one of the smaller enclosures.

And though I can't help smiling as I take in the nest it made with Jake's T-shirt, the one he'd surrendered straight off his back, the only way we could get the young raccoon to stop its sad mewing and settle in for the night, my overriding emotion right now is concern. I was sure I'd find Jake in here.

Backtracking, I pad silently toward the living room, then past it to the kitchen. Draw up short at what I find. Because there, lit only by the weak moonlight filtering in through the window, is the man I love. And everything is most definitely not okay.

A lump grows in my throat as I stand there, feeling like a voyeur as I stare at him where he sits in nothing but his boxer briefs, his head cradled in his hands as he hunches over the table. So many words form on my lips, but they all wither and fade before they have a chance to be spoken.

Jake wouldn't want me to catch him like this. Whatever it is that's happening, I don't want to make it worse.

I feel my pulse fluttering beneath the thin skin of my neck as I back away, not stopping until I'm at the head of the hallway. I clear my throat softly. Then call out into the night.

"Jake?"

His voice sounds startled and anxious as he answers. "Yeah. In here."

This time, when I reach the kitchen, he's sitting up. He gives me a wan smile, one that doesn't reach his eyes.

"Is everything okay?"

His lips twitch. "Everything's fine. I just couldn't sleep."

It's a first. Since we started sharing a bed, Jake's always fallen asleep right away while I lie awake for hours battling insomnia, dark thoughts, and even darker memories.

I enter the kitchen warily, approaching slowly like he's a wild animal I might scare off.

"Do you want to talk about it?"

"There's nothing to talk about."

I remember reading an article once that suggested that if you needed to have an important conversation with a man, it was better to do it in a situation where he wouldn't feel pressured to make eye contact, like while you're sitting side by side in a car. That won't work now, but I have another idea.

Walking behind him, I curl my hands over his shoulders and start kneading his muscles, surprised by how many knots I find. Though he tenses at my initial touch, by degrees, he relaxes until his rigid posture and the strained tendons along the sides of his neck are gone.

He leans back against me. Slips his hands over mine. Though I hate to undo all my hard work, now that he's unwound a bit, I have to know.

"Is this about your mom?"

In an instant, the knots are back. His voice is equally tight as he says, "No."

"It's okay to be upset. You know that, don't you? It doesn't matter what she's done. She's still you're family."

"I'm not upset about Janine. She's right where she

needs to be."

The way he says it suggests otherwise. Rounding his chair, I prop myself against the table in front of him. "Then what are you upset about?"

"Nothing."

"Jake—"

"Seriously, Cassie. I'm not going to say something just because it's what you want to hear. Sometimes I wish you'd just back off."

My head reels back. He's never spoken to me so sharply before. And though I know I'm overreacting, I can't help it.

Tears sting my eyes. I blink rapidly, trying not to let them fall, but as he stands so abruptly that his chair tips over, I lose the battle. One slips over my lower lid and trickles down my skin until it falls off the cliff of my jaw.

His face crumples.

"I didn't mean to snap at you."

His touch is soft as he cups a hand to my cheek. The kiss that follows is even softer. But almost before it starts, it's over.

I catch his arm as he pulls away. "Stay."

"I've got to get some sleep."

My chest aches as he steps around the table. I feel like I've been gutted with a plastic spoon. A second tear escapes, then a third. The sound of his steps is fading. He's almost left the room. If I'm going to do something, it needs to be soon.

"I'm sorry," I say, voice breaking over the words.

He stops.

"For what?"

"For whatever I've done to make you so mad at me."

"Cassie, I'm not mad at you."

I give him a look over my shoulder that lets him

know I don't believe him. Turn my head away as a fresh volley of tears begins to fall.

Then he's standing in front of me again, though he's so blurry I can't see his expression. His thumbs gently dry under my eyes. "Please don't cry."

"Then don't lie."

"I'm not." He wraps his arms around me, pulling me close, holding me against his chest. His face nestles in my hair, muffling his voice as he says, "I'm not going to say that I don't get annoyed by how reckless you can be, but it's not you I'm angry with. It's the guy who hit you today. The one who shot at you last night. And all the rest of the people lining up to try and hurt you. But mostly it's with myself."

"Why?" I ask, not understanding.

"Because I should be doing more to protect you. To keep you safe. And every time something like this happens, I feel like I'm failing."

Shaking my head, I pull back until I can see him.

"It's not your job to keep me safe."

"And it's not yours to get me to talk about my feelings."

"What else is there to do?" I joke, wiping at my eyes and sniffing.

"I can think of a few things."

The look in his eyes is hungry, but the kiss that follows is downright ravenous. I wrap my legs around his waist as he unties the belt on my bathrobe. Shiver as he guides the sleeves down my shoulders, his fingertips leaving goosebumps in their wake.

I tell my mind to be quiet. Try to focus on how his touch feels rather than the worries that plague me. Do my best to enjoy the moment as he lifts me from the table and carries me to the bedroom.

Given everything we've been through lately, it's understandable that we're both on edge. Frustrated. Worried. That our tempers are short and our nerves are frayed.

It's quite possible that my desire to make him open up to me stems from a desperate need to gain control over as much as possible in my life right now. I should respect that while all the stress makes me yearn to be closer to Jake, it might have him wanting more space, instead. Maybe the disconnect I'm experiencing stems more from my own insecurities rather than a problem between us that actually exists.

But I just can't shake the feeling that he's hiding something. And if I'm right, considering the lengths he'll go to in order to hide it, I'm afraid to find out what.

CHAPTER 11

I should have known better. Until now, it's been such a quiet, peaceful day, but as a shadow falls over my shoulder, blocking out the sun, it's clear that's going to change. My skin draws tight. My heart thumps hard against the ground beneath me, like it's trying to punch a hole in the earth for me to hide in. All I can think is, I should have known better than to be in such a vulnerable position.

I continue staring at the page I was reading, though I no longer see the words on my Kindle screen. I have to remain calm. I have to keep it together. I have to conceal my fear.

Slowly, I turn my head until I can see the figure looming over me. Like an eclipse, the body has been cast in darkness, the face nothing but a dark outline against the bright sky, but what I can tell is, it's a man. Tall, like Jake. Not as broad, but still muscular.

I set my Kindle down, freeing my hands. Place my palms on either side of me. Keep an eye on the intruder as I push my torso up off the blanket and swing my legs around until I'm in a sitting position.

If this person knew who I was and intended to harm me, they wouldn't have allowed me to do that. Because now, if I have to draw my weapon, it's going to be a lot easier to aim before I fire. Which I really want to do.

Whoever this is, they're uninvited. They've hiked halfway across the paddock to find me. And the way they're just standing, staring at me without saying a word, is giving me the creeps. Then the man shifts his weight, and like a magician waving a wand, his face is revealed.

"Julian?" I ask, squinting up at Jake's colleague, the other senior partner at the corporate law firm of Myers and Kleinman. "What are you doing here?"

"The real question is, what are you doing to Jake?"

I open my mouth to snap a response. We've been over this before. Only, before I bark my reply, I realize that this time he didn't ask what I was doing *with* Jake, but *to* him. Icy fingers prickle up my spine at the implication.

"What do you mean?"

"I mean, this whole thing with you testifying against his mom. It's messing with his head."

"How so? What's he said?"

"He hasn't said anything."

"Then how—"

"Because I've worked with the guy for over a decade and in all that time, he's raised his voice on maybe half a dozen occasions, all of which were warranted. But I just saw him completely ream out an intern this morning for a tiny mistake. One that was understandable, considering it's not the kind of law we do."

"What do you mean by—? Sit down, you're making me nervous." I wait until he's settled reluctantly on the blanket beside me. He runs his hands over the legs of his slacks, eyeing the grass like it's a creature he's never seen before and he's worried it might spit. Turning to face him, I say, "Explain reamed. What exactly did he do?"

Julian stares at me with a shocked look on his face. He reaches up and touches his own cheek, mirroring where my bruise is.

"What happened? Did Jake—?"

"What? No! Jake would never."

"Then what?"

"I interrupted a meth head robbing a pharmacy."

His expression is unreadable as he gives me a long look. Finally, he says, "It's like you're a magnet for trouble."

"You're not the first person to tell me that. Now, I want to hear about what Jake did. He yelled at an intern?"

Julian presses his lips together in a way that suggests he wishes he hadn't said anything. "Maybe I was wrong. Maybe he was just upset because you got hurt."

"But Jake yelled?"

Julian nods.

"What did the intern do wrong? You said Jake had them working on something that involved a different form of law. What kind?"

"It's nothing."

"You came here because you thought it was. So tell me."

He looks away, frowning as he says, "It was the contract for his mother's new counsel."

"He's hiring her a new lawyer?"

"Yes. A whole team of them, actually."

I don't know what to say. Or how to feel. All the times Jake said he wasn't upset about his mom, that she deserves what she gets—were those all lies? My stomach gurgles as I shift on the blanket, trying to ease the sharp sensation of having had a knife lodged between my shoulder blades.

"I was surprised. I mean, not just because of you two, but because after he spoke with his dad—"

"Wait. He spoke with his father?"

"Yes."

"And told you about it?"

But not me. That makes even less sense than hiring a defense team for his mom. He hates his dad. Refuses to be in the same room with him. The one time I suggested he give the man a chance to make amends, he shot the idea down so fast I practically got whiplash.

It's almost like Julian and I are talking about two different people. Or maybe just the two different faces the same man shows each of us. The thought makes me feel ill.

"Do you know what his dad told him?"

"To forget about his mom. That he was better off without her."

And yet, that's not what Jake decided to do, is it?

"Is that thing safe?" Julian asks.

I follow his finger to where he's pointing at the raccoon, the kit walking across the blanket toward me. This morning, after the vet examined her—as I suspected, the sanctuary's newest rescue is a girl—I brought her out here, under a tree in the paddock to play and get some fresh air. Though she'd climbed up onto a low bough to sleep, it appears that naptime is over.

The more time I spend with her, the more convinced I become that she's somebody's pet. The way she climbs into my lap now uninvited, and curls up, making herself comfortable, further supports this theory.

"I think so. But I've only known her for about twenty-four hours."

"And you aren't… worried?"

Not about the raccoon, but I can't say the same about Jake.

"She's fine. She won't touch you."

I stroke the raccoon's back absently, frowning into space. What's Jake's goal? What does he intend to achieve by hiring a new defense team for his mother? The answer seems obvious, and yet, hadn't he told me just last night that prison was where she needs to be? It doesn't make any sense.

Unless Julian is lying. My gaze slides sideways to where the man sits.

"Why are you telling me this?"

"I don't know. Maybe I shouldn't have. I'm just trying to… be a friend, I guess."

To me or to Jake? And to what end? Though I don't know this man well, my past experience with him suggests that he only takes actions that he stands to benefit from.

So what is it that he hopes to gain? Is he here to try to drive a wedge into my relationship with Jake? Or to tell me that, like my own gut keeps saying, the man I love is struggling right now?

Julian leans forward, peering into the distance. "Is that one of those mini goats?"

Stephano must have just now realized we have a visitor, because he's dancing across the paddock toward us.

"Yes. And I'm warning you, he already considers you his property."

I watch as the tiny goat frolics directly over to Julian, puts his front hooves on the man's knee with total disregard for what are probably very expensive trousers, sticks his tongue out, and *baas* at him.

"Is this… does this mean he likes me?"

"Hey, what's going on?"

I flinch, startled. Replay Jake's voice in my mind as I look over my shoulder at him, forcing a smile. Had he sounded stressed? Upset? No. I'm fairly certain that tightness in his tone was suspicion.

"I saw your car parked out front," he says to Julian.

He'd seen Julian's car, didn't know where either of us was, and yet he's wearing jeans and a T-shirt, so he obviously took the time to change before finding out. That's not like him.

"What's the occasion?" he asks. "It isn't like you to make house calls."

He takes a seat close beside me, one arm stretched almost possessively across my back, hand braced on the blanket. Though I turn toward him for a kiss, he doesn't seem to notice, his steely gaze still fixed on Julian.

"I was looking for you, man," Julian says. "Didn't know where you went after you took off earlier. I thought I'd find you here."

"And when you didn't, what?" There's a challenge in Jake's voice.

Julian shifts uncomfortably. He puts a hand on Stephano to keep the goat from climbing onto his lap. "I figured you'd show up eventually, so I thought I'd wait."

"Well, I'm here now. What do you need?"

Julian's eyes flit between me and Jake. He clears his throat. "I have that, uh, paperwork you were worried about earlier. In my car. I know you were in a rush to get it executed."

Jake's expression softens as he nods. "Thanks. I appreciate that."

Something at my core clenches. If Julian's talking about the contract for Jake's mother's new lawyers, that means Julian was telling me the truth. And that he doesn't want Jake to know he told me.

Suddenly, I'm exhausted. I lean back against Jake's arm, resting my head against his shoulder. It's only then, when I feel how rigid his muscles are beneath me, that I realize how tense he truly is. But why?

Because he's upset that Julian and I were here alone, talking on a blanket? Because he's worried that I'll find out about the lawyers he's hiring to defend his mom? Or is there something else—something worse—that he's keeping from me?

CHAPTER 12

It's funny. Fear makes you sharpen your senses. Anger makes you sharpen your claws. But apparently, worry dulls your everything and makes you clumsy.

The raccoon watches from inside her crate in the corner as I chase the onion across the kitchen. Luckily, I haven't peeled it yet, so no harm's been done. The same can't be said about the glass I broke earlier. Or the half pot of cooked pasta that's now in the trash because I spilled it onto the floor.

Though Jake has seemed to relax since Julian left and we came inside to make dinner, my own nerves have done nothing but grow worse. I'm not sure what it is that I'm missing, or even if there's anything to really miss. My gut screams that there is but… maybe it's wrong. Maybe I'm blowing things out of proportion, or just being paranoid.

After all, how many times have I told Jake that it's okay to be upset about his mom? To want to help her? Or to give his dad a second chance?

But that's exactly it. I've done my best to make it clear that I'm okay with however he chooses to deal with the family strife he's dealing with. And yet, he's snuck around behind my back, hiding his interactions with them both.

It feels like a betrayal.

I'm not sure what to believe, think, do. And this whole not trusting my own instincts thing is tying me up in knots.

I want to talk to him about it. Give him an opportunity to explain. But I'm afraid. What if he denies it, or tells me it's none of my business, or any of the dozens of other responses that would feel like a dagger to my heart? I'm the person he's supposed to discuss these things with, yet it seems I'm the only one he's not confiding in right now.

My phone rings and I jerk, startled, dropping the onion again and almost stabbing myself with the knife I was using to chop it. Cursing, I set the blade down and snatch the bulb from the floor. Rinse it under the tap as I answer my cell.

"Hello?"

"Agent Knox, hey. Is everything all right?"

Agent Gellar's voice makes those knots inside me draw just a teeny bit tighter.

"Yeah, why?"

"I don't know. You sound tense."

I force a laugh. It sounds as fake as it feels. "I just dropped dinner."

"Oh no. Should I let you go?"

"No. I need a break. What's up?"

I take a seat. My legs bounce so violently that the table's at risk of being knocked across the room.

"They identified the sniper who tried to shoot you."

A burning sensation starts in my chest, a bubble of acid lodging under my sternum. I rub at it absently.

"Who was he?"

"His name was Don Farris. Claimed to be a handyman, filed as an independent contractor on his taxes, though I don't think the kind of odd jobs he undertook are what the IRS had in mind."

Thinking of the weapon he'd used, the Mil-Spec modifications that had been made to it, I ask, "Military background?"

"Surprisingly, no."

"Are they able to tie him to Bianchi?"

"Not directly, but they run in the same circles. Given that the man's been known to perform dirty work for several of the larger drug traffickers in South Florida, it seems likely that Bianchi's the one who ordered the hit."

It's nothing I didn't expect, but for some reason, having it confirmed makes me feel a million times worse.

"So what do we do now?"

"That's what I'm calling to discuss. I'm planning to request that they increase their surveillance of him at the prison where he's being held. And that they also restrict his communication, but…"

My breath comes quicker. "But what?"

"But I wanted to speak to you first. His legal team is sure to fight against it. They'll claim there's no proof that he's the one who ordered the attack on you. And they're right."

"Which means he's free to keep soliciting killers." My vision tunnels, a red tinge clouding the edges.

Agent Gellar neither confirms nor denies my statement, but she doesn't need to. We both know it's true.

"Listen, Cassidy… Have you considered witness

protection?"

"No." I smack the table to accentuate my point as I say, "Absolutely not."

"It wouldn't be forever. Just until after you testify at his trial."

"His trial isn't for months. I'm not the criminal here. Why should I have to be the one to disrupt my life?"

"I agree it isn't fair."

"It's more than that." My voice shakes with the words. My whole body is trembling. "We both know that they don't need my testimony to get a conviction. Which means even if the court excused me, this wouldn't be over. He's not after me to keep me silent. This is about revenge."

"It's possible that you're right."

Squeezing my eyes shut, I struggle to stay calm, but it's a battle I'm close to losing. All the deep breathing in the world isn't going to help. My insides are at a rapid boil.

"So then, what this really means is that in order to stay safe, I'd have to stay in WITSEC until Bianchi's execution. That's only, what? Twenty years away, with appeals?"

"I agree that this isn't ideal—"

"It's more than just 'not ideal,'" I snap. Shooting a look toward the doorway, I lower my voice, and say, "WITSEC is not an option. Period. There's got to be another way."

"Well, if you think of one, I'm all ears."

I'm at risk of biting through my tongue, so I release it from between my gritted teeth. Spit out a wry, "Thanks." Swallowing down the curse words that want to follow, I ask, "Is there anything else?"

"No."

"Then I appreciate the update. I've got to go."

I don't give her an opportunity to reply before I hang up, ending the call. Tears of frustration sting my eyes. I glare at my hands, clenched into fists on the table before me, until they reabsorb.

I'm not going to allow this to happen. I don't care what lines I have to cross, what I have to do, I'm not going to live the rest of my life in fear—or have it shortened by some hitman.

Unfurling my fingers, ignoring the half-moons weeping blood on my palms, I think about what it is that Bianchi has that's enabling him to do this. Power. Wealth. Life. If it means saving myself and the future I have planned? I'll find a way to take all of those things from him.

CHAPTER 13

I've suffered a lot of injuries over the course of my life. I've been hit, strangled, branded, abused in a number of ways. This is as painful as any of those things. Yet I keep coming back. Even though I have to because the Bureau requires it for me to keep receiving a paycheck, I still suspect that makes me a masochist.

Dr. Evangeline sits across from me in an overstuffed chair. Today she's wearing a tailored pantsuit in her signature color, white. Pure, spotless white. As usual, I inspect her outfit, looking for a mark, a stain, anything that would suggest she's the same species of human as me. But as usual, she's flawless.

"I saw your picture in the paper," she says.

I freeze. As far as I know, there wasn't a story about me after the sniper attack. It's possible that I might have missed it, but if I did, I need to find out what it says. What it reveals. What key piece of information some reporter might have inadvertently provided the next hitman that could improve their odds of success.

Or maybe I'm worrying about nothing. Surely someone would have said something if it were true. And I haven't been here for almost a month, not since I was placed on medical leave yet again after my most recent run-in with a serial killer. It's possible the picture she's referring to appeared closer to our last appointment than this one.

But thinking about the most recent photograph of me that I'm aware had been printed, one where I'm sitting outside the shed where I'd been held captive, an incident I'd used to buy me as much time off from these weekly sessions as I was able, doesn't make me feel much better.

"Your boyfriend was in it too. He's very attractive, isn't he?"

Exhaling with relief, I smile. She must be talking about the shot of Jake and me attending the annual Myers and Kleinman gala.

"I think so."

She smirks in a way that suggests I just made the understatement of the year. I toss one right back at her because I'm feeling belligerent and fractious and maybe even a bit like I want to start a fight, even though it's probably not a good idea to go to war with your therapist.

"That was a gorgeous dress you were wearing."

"Is this what the Bureau's paying you to talk to me about? Fashion?"

"To be honest? No. I'm sure they'd much rather that I was still trying to get you to discuss your time in Harold Griggs' basement. Or how it felt to be kidnapped by a killer who tried to recreate that scenario for you."

Oh. So she did see that picture. And read the accompanying article, apparently.

Dr. Evangeline sighs heavily.

"Listen, Cassidy. I know you don't want to be here. I get it. For some people, being forced to talk about their feelings is just as painful as the trauma that caused them. And I'm going to be honest with you."

I tuck my hands under the backs of my thighs, digging my nails in deep, bracing myself for what she's about to say.

"I don't think you need to be here. I think you're just fine."

That's the last thing I was expecting to hear. Turns out, she isn't as perfect as I thought, because she's wrong.

"I know some time has passed since our last session, but after what happened to you, I'd expect you to be a wreck right now. Yet you're not."

Or I've just become a very good actress. Because while it's true that I wasn't completely re-traumatized by being kidnapped and handcuffed to a pole in a room designed to recreate the experience I had of being held by now-infamous serial killer Harold Griggs, I'm not okay.

My nightmares occur with even more frequency. I can still feel the hot breath of a panic attack on the back of my neck entirely too often. And though I've never been what you'd call a trusting person, now I have downright issues, suspecting people and their motives more than ever before.

"So I want to propose something new," the doctor continues. "Since you have to keep coming to these appointments for a while, why don't we try to make this more enjoyable for you? We can sit and chat, like friends. Or even just strangers in line at the grocery store. Or, we can go back to me asking you questions you don't want to answer. It's your call. Which would you prefer?"

I have no doubt that she's up to something. That there's some kind of ulterior motive at play here. But am I really going to pass up an opportunity to not be picked at like a peeling scab? To seize whatever control over these sessions that I can manage, even if it means walking into some kind of headshrinking trap?

I don't think I could make myself resist the offer no matter how hard I tried. I'll just have to watch my step and do my best not to reveal anything I don't want to. So basically, the only thing that's changing is that instead of asking what she wants to know outright, she'll have to work harder to try to trip me up. Works for me.

Clearing my throat, I say, "I think that talking like friends would be nice. Thank you."

She gives me what's perhaps the first genuine smile I've seen since we started these sessions. "Great. Now. Would you like to discuss your dress? Or is there something else you'd like to talk about?"

Even though she's just cut me what feels like the deal of a lifetime, I'm still not sure I like this woman. And I know I don't trust her. But is that because I always expect the worst from people? She certainly hasn't done anything to merit it.

It's possible that I'm letting my suspicions cloud the situation. If she's offering an olive branch here, maybe I should take it. Because there *is* something I desperately need to talk about, but it can't be with someone who knows Jake, which excludes anyone I'd normally speak to.

"Actually…" I draw it out, trying to buy time to change my mind. To my surprise, my resolve sticks, even after Dr. Evangeline leans forward in her seat like she's preparing to hear some juicy gossip. And then I see it. A small makeup smear on the collar of her jacket. Maybe she's human after all.

So I take the leap and ask, "Do you remember me telling you how I'd discovered that Jake's mom had helped murder my parents?"

"That's kind of a hard thing to forget."

"Well, she just had her first pretrial hearing. At least, she was supposed to, but it was delayed. That's beside the point, though. Jake and I were there. And, well, I'm not sure he's okay."

"It's understandable for him to be upset."

"I know. And I've told him that. But he keeps insisting he's not."

"Plenty of men keep their feelings bottled inside."

"It's more than just that. He's hiding things."

"What kinds of things?"

"He's hiring a defense team for his mom. Which is fine. I understand."

"So what's the problem?"

"He's not the one who told me. A coworker of his did."

"Hmm."

"And supposedly he lost his temper with an intern, which is completely out of character for him."

"Anything else?"

"He spoke with his father."

Dr. Evangeline's expression makes it clear that she doesn't understand why that would be an issue. And telling her feels like a betrayal of Jake's trust. But he's betrayed my trust. Besides, it's not like she can share anything I tell her with anyone else.

Just to be sure, I ask, "Everything we say stays in this room, just between us, right?"

"With the exception of you telling me something that made me believe you intend to harm yourself or someone else, yes, you're correct."

I make a mental note where to draw the line on what I confess to her, then say, "Jake's dad is an alcoholic. A rather abusive one. After his mom abandoned them, it got… really bad. He still has scars from the beatings he took as a child."

My gaze drifts out the window to where a blue jay hops across a patch of grass, looking for food.

"And he was never removed from his home? DCF never intervened?"

"No."

She makes a sound of disapproval. I ignore it and forge ahead.

"I, um, spoke with his father, not long ago. While I was there, he asked me to tell Jake that he'd like the opportunity to apologize. He wanted the chance to try to repair their relationship."

"And you told Jake that?"

"Yes."

"How'd he take it?"

"Not well."

"And your concern is…"

"If he has no interest in repairing his relationship with his father, why did he go talk to him? And then not tell me about it?"

"I do see how that could be frustrating."

"But considering the context, everything else that's been going on, don't you think I should be worried?"

"Have you talked to him about it?"

"No."

"You probably should."

"I know. It's just… why didn't he tell me? It's not like I would have been upset. Certainly not like finding out secondhand. Every time I open my mouth to say something—about any of it—I think that if he wanted me to know, he'd have told me himself."

"It's likely that's true."

My mouth goes dry, my tongue like sandpaper as I ask, "So then you *don't* think I should talk to him?"

"I didn't say that, either."

I bite the inside of my cheek to keep from screaming. Keep my hands away from my hair so I don't pull it out. Watch as she shifts in her seat, not meeting my gaze as she fidgets with the pen lying on the table beside her.

"Sometimes, the most important things we have to say are hardest to discuss with the people we love. It could be because we don't want them to think we're weak, or don't want to disappoint them, or an endless variety of other reasons. But something of this magnitude?"

She leans forward and touches my hand. I'm shocked by the gesture, a lump of emotion forming in my throat.

"I can see how much this is bothering you, Cassidy. So my advice—as both a friend and a therapist—would be to confront him. Calmly. Hear him out. Be patient and don't judge. Secrets like this are only going to grow until they come between you."

I swallow hard, knowing that she's right. But there's another possibility, one I'm even more afraid of. Because sometimes secrets are glue and it's the truth that tears you apart.

CHAPTER 14

The sky outside my car is dark and ominous. The gathering clouds have a heavy look, like they're full of damaging secrets they're waiting to spill. Pressure builds as the developing downpour fails to unleash its fury.

But the storm I fear has nothing to do with the weather.

I have to do something. I can't just sit around, hoping, waiting, driving myself crazy. The stakes are too high. I have to take action.

It's just too bad that the only place I can think of to go for answers is one of the last I should visit, because I'm going anyway, ignoring the common sense that tells me I shouldn't.

There's no denying that the decision has made me tense, my hands tightening on the steering wheel until my muscles ache. My heart hammers erratically. My breath is quick and shallow. And when my cell phone trills as I receive an incoming call, I jump in my seat.

"Hello?"

"Hi, I got your message. Is everything all right?"

Though my boss's voice usually has the ability to soothe my frayed nerves, this time it doesn't. If anything, it makes them worse. I want to yell. To cry. To scream. Instead, my voice is eerily low and even.

"I don't think so. No."

"Tell me everything."

How many times have I done exactly that? Offloaded on Marla? And though all the words I long to say are right there, on the tip of my tongue, I bite them back. Swallow them down.

I can't confess the problems I feel brewing between me and Jake. Though I want her comfort and reassurance, that's not the most pressing need I'm faced with right now. Because the first step toward fixing whatever's wrong is to take back my life, and I'm not sure I can do that alone. At least, not without some information first.

"I need a favor."

"Okay. I'll see what I can do. What is it?"

"They identified the sniper who shot at me. His name was Don Farris."

"That's great news. Isn't it?"

I make a noncommittal noise. "According to Agent Gellar, they can't make any direct connection between him and Tony Bianchi."

"Even if one exists, it might not be possible to confirm, Cassidy."

"I understand. And I realize that the intel they do have establishing ties between him and Bianchi's peers in the drug trade is almost the same thing."

"But?"

"I need more. Exact names. Instances. Known accomplices. The type of beer he drinks. His mother's shoe size."

"So, all the things."

"*All* of them," I emphasize. "Most of all, I want to know how this guy found his jobs. If there's some kind of middleman, or handler, or a job board where lowlifes advertise that they're looking for hitmen. If Bianchi didn't hire him directly, I need to figure out who he has on the outside doing his dirty work for him."

Director Jacobson clears her throat. "What do you plan on doing with this information once you have it?"

Silence stretches between us as I struggle for an answer. Finally, I admit, "I don't know. I'm not sure yet. Maybe nothing."

"Or maybe—?" she prods.

"Maybe I'll discover something that will help me keep Bianchi from trying to come at me again."

I have no idea what that something might be, or how I could leverage it in my favor, but I have to look for it all the same, because if it's there, I'll find it. For most of my fifteen years with the FBI, that's what I did—search for patterns. And I excelled at it. Now, I need to use those skills to help myself.

Because I have to believe that it was the attempt on my life that's caused the shift between me and Jake, and not anything to do with his mother. The issue is, I no longer have access to the databases I need to find this information out on my own, which means I really need to convince Marla to help me.

"Cassidy," Director Jacobson's voice is gentle. I brace myself for what's coming next, knowing I won't like it. "Maybe you should leave this for the Miami field office to handle. Come back up here for a little while. Just until things calm down."

How can I explain that that's not an option without

sounding crazy? That there's a twisting sensation in my gut telling me that if I don't handle this myself—and quickly—that I could lose what I hold most dear? How could she possibly understand, when I don't myself?

"I… wish I could, Marla."

I hold my breath, waiting for her to counter with the question: why can't I? But thankfully, it doesn't come. She knows me. Which is why I should have anticipated the question she *does* ask.

"Is there something you aren't telling me?"

Exhaling heavily, I fill my lungs with fresh air. I don't want to lie to her, but I can't share the truth.

"Let me rephrase that. On a scale of one to ten, how deadly is this secret you're keeping?"

I consider the answer. While the possibility of losing Jake might feel like the end of the world, in reality, I know I'd survive it. But the people who caused the fracture between us? I'm not so sure what their fate would be.

"To me? Zero."

"Do I want to know who's at risk?"

"No."

There's a moment of prolonged silence before she says, "You're probably right. But can you do me one favor?"

"What's that?"

"Give me some advance warning if you're going to need bail money, okay?"

She says it with a laugh, but we both know she's serious.

"I'll try."

"That's all I can ask. I'll bring Mallory in on this and see what we can find out for you."

I thank her, but as the call ends, I find myself not

feeling better, but worse. Like I've just dragged one more person into the undertow with me. And as I turn off the main road onto the narrow dirt lane leading into the swamp, I know I'm about to get sucked in even deeper.

Because while there's a difference between making a deal with a devil and simply talking to one, I'm not so sure that Jake would see it. Not where this particular devil is concerned. And to be completely honest, I'm not so sure I see that difference, either.

CHAPTER 15

It's not too late to change my mind. To turn around. To escape. But the problem with that is, where is there to go? If I run away from this particular hell, I'd just be running toward another. At least here I know what to expect.

Still, adrenaline hums beneath my skin as I exit my vehicle. My legs feel shaky as I climb the front stairs. The last time I found myself on this doorstep, I was looking for a killer. Now? I find myself even more afraid of what I might discover inside.

That doesn't stop me from raising my hand. Making a fist. Knocking. Breathing a sigh equal parts dread and relief as the fiberglass stops rattling beneath my knuckles when it opens. And as it does, the storm breaks.

A flash of lightning streaks the sky, morphing the face before me into a grotesque mask of shadow and light. A strong hand grasps me by the forearm, yanking me inside. I stumble over the threshold into the darkened interior of the trailer.

"You all right? Hold on, I'll get you a towel."

I stay where I am until the man returns a moment later. Instead of handing me the towel, he drapes it around my shoulders with an odd sort of tenderness. Passes me another one, gesturing to my hair.

When I make no move to dry myself off, instead staring numbly at the dry fabric in my hand as if I've forgotten its use, he frowns. Cups a hand around my elbow and gently guides me toward the kitchen.

"Come on. Let's get you a drink to warm you up."

Reaching into my purse, I pull out a bottle and offer it to him. He grins. If there's one sure way to make a friend out of Dylan Walker, it's buying him a drink. Buying him a whole bottle? That's even better.

"I've been wanting to thank you," he says as he turns toward the cabinet, pulling out a clean glass. "I don't know what you said to get Jake to give me a chance, but whatever it was, I appreciate it."

I take a seat. He breaks the seal on the whiskey I brought, but before he has a chance to pour me a drink, I've removed a second fifth from my purse. Removing the cap, I drink straight from the bottle. His eyebrows rise with something like concern as he settles into the chair across from me.

"Is something wrong?" he asks.

I shrug and take another sip, not wanting to admit that *everything* is.

"You going to be okay to drive if you drink that?"

"I'll wait it off in the car if I'm not."

"You'll do no such thing. You know you're always welcome here, right?"

When I don't respond, he frowns down at his glass, then reluctantly pushes it to the side. It's not anything I ever expected to see.

"Why don't you tell me what's bothering you?"

"What makes you think anything is?"

"Because you're acting odder than a purple cat on a date with an orange mouse." He clears his throat. "Is it Jake?"

I tip my head back, filling my mouth with another glug from my bottle. Apparently, that's answer enough.

"Does he know you're here?"

"No."

"You want to keep this visit between you and me?"

"You'd do that?"

"Why wouldn't I?"

"I don't know. I wouldn't want you risking that second chance he's giving you."

Dylan rubs a hand over his face. "I wouldn't want that, either. But you're my best friends' little girl. And the reason my boy gave me that chance in the first place. So whatever you need..."

I shake my head. Swallow hard. Blink rapidly to contain the tears filling my eyes.

"Aw, sweetheart."

Dylan gets up and rounds the table. His knees crack as he crouches by my side, wrapping an arm awkwardly around my shoulders.

It's strange, to think that this man trying to comfort me right now is the same one who left the marks that still scar Jake's back. I know I shouldn't trust him. And yet, at the same time, I long to turn toward him and bury my head in his shoulder.

But I can't.

Instead, I wipe my eyes dry and draw a deep breath. Force a small smile.

"I'm fine, thank you."

"You sure?"

"Yes."

He looks like he doesn't believe me, but he stands with a muffled groan and returns to his seat, where he sits, studying me with an anguished expression.

"What?" I ask.

His voice cracks as he tries to speak. Pressing his lips tight together, he lifts a finger to his face, to the spot where a bruise mars the skin under my eye, visible despite my best efforts to conceal it with makeup. This time, it's his eyes that water. He looks away as his face turns red.

Clearing his throat, he whispers, "Did my boy do that? Is that why you're here?"

"No."

"No, he didn't do it? Or no, that's not why you're here?"

"No to both," I say.

"Thank God." He releases a weary sigh, his eyes rising to the ceiling before his gaze returns to mine. "He get in trouble for dealing out some justice to whoever did do it, then?"

I shake my head.

"That's a shame."

"I got in the way of some meth head who decided to rob the pharmacy," I explain, feeling the need to defend Jake's lack of violence. "I doubt Sheriff Kingston's going to track him down. I'll just have to hope that life deals out some justice for me."

"Is that what has you so upset? Knowing that guy's still out there?"

Though it strikes me as kind of ridiculous that someone would think I'd be so upset because a man who merely hit me was still out on the streets, I suppose that would be enough for most people. People who weren't me. People who didn't have a sniper try to take them out on their own doorstep, or serial killers hold them hostage.

But as far as I'm aware, Jake's dad doesn't know that I'm a federal agent. Most of Gator Glade doesn't, and I have no plans to fill them in. But I also can't let Dylan think that's what's affecting me, no matter how much I might like to.

"No."

Dylan's frown deepens. "Darlin', I want to help, but you're gonna have to tell me what's wrong."

"I need to know what Jake said when he came to visit you."

"What do you mean? He didn't tell you?"

"He didn't even tell me about the visit."

"How'd you find out then?"

I don't want to betray Jake's trust, but I don't think I have a choice. If he's not going to tell me what's going on, I have to find someone who will, even if my stomach feels like I'm riding a roller coaster after winning an oyster-eating contest at the thought of what I'm about to do. Trying to distract myself, I start rubbing at the edge of the whiskey bottle's label with my thumb.

"One of his coworkers mentioned it to me. When he was telling me about some uncharacteristic behavior Jake's been exhibiting."

"And you think that's because he came to see me?"

"No."

A bit of the tension in his expression eases.

"He was acting fine until this week."

"Until Janine's hearing?"

"It's hard to say, exactly."

"What do you mean?"

"The night before, a sniper took a shot at me."

Dylan covers his mouth with his hand as he curses. He looks ill as he stares at me. "I told him."

I freeze. Don't blink, don't breathe, it feels like even my heart stops beating for the very long minute it takes me to compose myself. "What?"

"I told him not to trust Janine. That she had a mean streak, a vengeful side."

"Is that what the two of you talked about when he came to see you?"

He nods. "I kept trying to apologize to him, make amends and all that, and he kept turning the conversation back to his mother. Wanted to know all about her. Asked me more questions about that woman in thirty minutes than he had in thirty years."

My grasp tightens around the bottle in my hand until I'm afraid it's going to shatter. But I can't make myself relax my grip.

"What?" Dylan asks. "There's something else that happened that you're not telling me."

"I should go."

"I'm not so sure you should."

"Why not?"

"Because you'll be safer here."

"How's that?"

He rams a knuckle in his mouth and bites down. I can see the war going on inside him in his tense expression. His rigid posture. The bead of blood that seeps from between his skin and his teeth. Finally, he removes his hand from his mouth, not seeming to notice the red smear that's left behind as he wipes at the wound he gave himself.

"I'd like you to stay."

"I can't do that."

His voice is thick with emotion as he says, "I failed

your parents."

"You didn't know Janine was planning to kill them." It feels like a fist has clenched around my heart as I say the words.

"No, I didn't. But I knew she was angry at them. Jealous. Bitter that they were so happy when we weren't. Believe me, if I'd had any idea what she was planning… since I found out she was behind what happened, not a day has gone by where I haven't regretted not taking a closer look and seeing what was really there. I'll never forgive myself if I let the same happen to you."

He looks at his untouched glass of whiskey, his eyes full of desire. All he'd have to do is reach for the glass to take a sip. There's nobody stopping him. And yet, he abstains.

"I think that you might be in danger."

"From who? Janine?"

"Yes. Her… and my son."

"You can't really believe that Jake would ever hurt me."

"I'm not sure what to believe, but I do know that it's not worth the risk."

"There is no risk. Not from Jake."

Ignoring my words, he says, "You should stay here. It doesn't have to be for long, just until things cool down."

I push back from the table.

"If you don't want to do that, I have some money saved up. You can have it. Go take yourself on a nice vacation."

My chair scrapes across the floor as I stand.

"Cassidy, please."

"No. I'm not listening to this. It's absurd."

Turning my back, I pull the towels off myself and

toss them onto the counter.

"I know you don't want to hear what I'm saying, but you need to."

I hurry from the room, quickening my steps as he follows me. Opening the door, I find a landscape that matches what I'm feeling—dark clouds, violent wind, driving rain lashing at the earth. A maelstrom. I pause for only a second before entering the fray.

"Cassidy!"

Casting a last look in his direction as I unlock my car, I spot a terrified-looking Dylan Walker clinging to the threshold. He shouts to be heard over the storm.

"He kept arguing with me about her. Trying to convince me that she wasn't all bad. Trying to make me agree with him. When I wouldn't, he got angry and left."

Tearing my eyes from his, I yank the driver's door open and throw myself behind the wheel. But before I can get it shut, I hear one last thing.

"Think about the blood that's in his veins. Her blood. My blood. I just want you to be careful, is all."

Cranking the engine, I ram the car into gear and speed off down the driveway. But once the trailer's out of sight behind me, I stop. Opening the door, I spill out onto the ground on my hands and knees, my body lurching as my stomach empties.

Collecting myself, I perch on the sill of the car, opening my mouth to the rain and spitting to rid my mouth of the acrid taste of vomit. It's not the alcohol that made me sick—my whiskey bottle had been filled with tea, a ploy to make Dylan drop his guard. It's my newfound knowledge.

Jake only went to visit his dad to ask about his mom. To try defending the woman who murdered my parents. The woman whose legal defense he's now paying for.

As badly as I'd hoped that I was right and Jake's change in behavior was caused by fear, I now have to at least consider that I was wrong. Which means I need to speak with him. And this time, I have to do whatever it takes to get answers.

CHAPTER 16

When I was little, I remember how time took forever to pass. The weeks between Halloween and Christmas seemed like a lifetime. Even the hours between morning and night felt like an eternity. Time feels a bit like that again now as I pace the kitchen, waiting for Jake to get home.

I worked so hard to prepare myself. Organize my thoughts. Gather my nerve.

But he's late.

Now, the inner calm I struggled so hard to find has been replaced by alternating waves of worry and anger. What if he hasn't called because something bad has happened and he can't? Or what if nothing bad has happened and he's simply chosen not to call despite knowing that his silence would send me on a collision course with panic?

My feet ache from pacing, but every time I make myself sit, I hop right back up to look out the window, sure that I've heard his truck pull up. Checking the time on my phone again, I hold it up toward the ceiling where it gets an extra bar of reception. Open up the text thread between us, making sure that I haven't somehow missed his response to the last message I sent a half hour ago. I haven't.

But he has read the message, which means he's choosing to ignore me. Just like he's choosing to send my calls to voicemail. It doesn't necessarily mean that his loyalty is now with his mother over me, but the longer he remains silent, the stronger the thought takes hold.

Maybe he's not even coming home. Or at least not this one. For all I know he's at his condo right now. As impossible as I would have found all this to believe even this morning, now, I just don't know. I'm not sure I can trust myself to see my reality accurately anymore.

It makes my heart feel like it's been ripped out of my chest and shoved down a garbage disposal, dull, slimy blades mixing the organ with rotting food waste. Because as much as I want to love fiercely and blindly and with unwavering trust, I don't know if I can. I might not be capable.

I've spent my entire career faced with the harsh reality of what happens to women in this world. Women who turn the other cheek. Who only see what they want to. Who let their guard down for an instant.

As much as we all want to believe that it's strangers who pose the most danger, statistically, it's not. And while I could never imagine Jake ever doing anything to hurt me, that doesn't mean it's not possible.

A dull thud sounds from outside. I hurry to compose myself, using the camera on my phone to check my reflection. My eyes are tinged red and my skin is a bit blotchy, but it's not completely obvious that I've spent the last several hours fighting off tears. Forcing myself down into one of the chairs at the table, I wait.

There's a series of beeps from the keypad on the door, followed by the clunk of the deadbolt turning. Footsteps carry inside. A moment later, Jake appears.

"Hey." He hovers in the doorway, avoiding my eyes. He looks wrecked. My resolve to confront him wavers. "Sorry I'm late. I was in a meeting that ran over."

"Are you hungry?"

"No." Grabbing a glass from the cabinet, he fills it with water, takes a long sip before setting it on the counter by the sink. "I just want to grab a shower and get in bed."

I nod, weighing my options. Do I put off this conversation until tomorrow night, knowing that my thoughts will be torturing me the entire time? Or do I force the issue now, when he's obviously already in a bad mood?

Before I decide, the cup clinks, followed by a splash. Jake curses. Turning, I see the glass on its side, a puddle of water on the floor.

"I've got it," I say, standing.

Without a word he snatches the dishtowel I'm reaching for and crouches, attacking the floor. It looks like he's trying to scrub a hole through it more than mop up a spill. I guess we're doing this now after all.

Kneeling, I take his hand in mine, stilling his frantic wiping. "Jake, what's wrong?"

He pulls away, rising to his feet. "I wish you'd stop asking me that."

"And I wish you'd answer honestly," I say, taking my time as I stand beside him.

His jaw clenches. His nostrils flare. The muscles in his neck stand out like ropes pulled taut beneath his skin. "What makes you so sure I'm not?"

"Besides the way you've been acting?"

"I don't know what you're talking about."

I gesture toward him. "Are you really trying to say that you aren't on edge right now?"

"What? Because I cussed when I spilled some water?"

"Among other things."

"Like?"

I realize my mistake too late, because now I have to give him an example.

"Like yelling at an intern," I say softly.

He goes so still he no longer appears to be breathing. His eyes narrow. His voice is a low growl as he asks, "Who told you that? Julian?"

"Yes."

"What else did he tell you?"

"That something's wrong. That you've been acting upset."

"And you believe him? Over me?"

"In this case? I think that I do."

I've never seen the expression that now darkens Jake's face before. He mutters to himself as he storms by me. I follow him into the living room. Watch as he snatches his keys and wallet from the end table. Grabs his briefcase from the floor.

"Where are you going?" I ask.

"Anywhere but here."

"Seriously? You're just going to leave? You're not going to talk this out?"

"What do you expect, Cassidy?"

I stare at him, not sure I heard right. I don't think he's ever called me by my full name before, not once in almost thirty-nine years. But his expression makes it clear—I heard correctly.

Part of me wants to beg him not to go. Before that part can speak, the rest of me clamps my tongue painfully between my teeth, because this isn't all on me. I'm not trying to antagonize him. I'm trying to understand so that I can help.

I'm fighting for our relationship here, but it feels like I'm the only one. Which means that while 49% of me feels horrible regret, the other 51% is simmering with anger, the kind that makes me afraid of what might come out if I open my mouth.

So I watch him walk out the door. Listen for the sound of his truck engine as I stalk around the house like a tiger trying to reach its prey. But the sound doesn't come.

Would I hear it over the thundering rush of my pulse in my ears? Over my own voice filling my head with doubts and regrets? Over the crunch of my molars as they grind together?

It's likely, considering I catch the faint mewling coming from behind the closed door at the back of the house. Rushing down the hall, I fling the door open and turn on the light. The raccoon looks at me with sad eyes, reaching an arm toward me between the bars of her pen. The fight must have woken her.

Opening the door, I gather her in my arms. Murmur soft apologies as I gently rock her, hoping to get her back to sleep. As I do, I pull out my phone and check the surveillance camera app.

Jake is still parked out front. No doubt he's planning on spending the night sleeping in his truck, afraid to leave me alone to fend for myself against another attempt on my life.

He really does love me, we're just going through a rough patch right now. All couples have them. I just have to have faith that we'll get through it.

The hot coal inside the pit of my stomach cools a little. Sorrow takes its place.

If the situation had been reversed, and Jake had listened to another woman's opinion about how I was feeling over my own, how would I have felt? The flames of my fury probably would have been seen in space, that's how.

I owe him an apology. And as soon as I get the kit settled, I'm going to go out there and give him one.

Ten minutes later, she's back in the cage, curled up with Jake's shirt. Her eyes are closed. Her body rises and falls with deep breaths. Carefully, I tiptoe from the room and turn off the light.

Then I race to the front door and fling it open. My throat squeezes tight. The tears I've been battling all day finally win, cascading down my cheeks.

Jake's gone. He left me after all.

CHAPTER 17

Everything feels wrong. My skin is too tight, my nerves too frayed, my heart too heavy. And my brain? It doesn't believe what's going on. But it's true.

Last night, when I first realized Jake had left, I was convinced something bad must have happened to him. I even brought up the surveillance footage, sure that I'd see a gunman approach Jake's truck and force him to drive away. When that didn't prove true, I rewound the video even farther, watching the vehicle from the moment he got home to make sure someone hadn't climbed inside, hidden in the back seat.

No one did.

Which means that despite everything that's been going on, the threat I might be facing, he chose to go. The Jake I know wouldn't do that. But how well do I really know him?

I've been back less than half a year. Sure, we were inseparable as children, but that was a long time ago.

Over thirty years. Before his mom helped murder my parents and abandoned him. The mom who he's decided to buy a legal defense for, to help her get away with what she did to my family.

Emptying the last three Tums from the plastic bottle, I crunch them between my aching molars, wondering if I'm a fool. But I refuse to give up just yet. Even my grandfather, the man who raised me to be so wary and on guard, trusted Jake implicitly. I can't allow myself to be a coward and turn my back on what we have just because it turns out he's human and not perfect.

All night long, I kept telling myself to give him the benefit of the doubt and not jump to conclusions. As I paced around the house. Checked in on the sleeping raccoon, selfishly wanting to wake her for a cuddle. As I desperately tried to get some sleep.

But every time I closed my eyes, I saw Jake's back as he walked through the door without a backward glance. The harder I tried to clear my mind, the louder Dylan Walker's parting words rang inside it: *"Think about the blood that's in his veins. Her blood."*

My heart is begging me not to rush to conclusions. My gut keeps assuring me that there's an explanation.

At the same time, I'm so hurt that I can't help being angry. Would he have left if he really cared about me?

Even if he would, is this what I have to look forward to in this relationship? Him taking off instead of staying and talking it out like an adult whenever I do something that upsets him? He's the one who felt the need to sneak around, even though I've done my best to let him know that it wasn't necessary.

Which brings me around to the entire *how well do I really know him* argument again. Maybe we're moving too fast. Maybe this is my sign that I need to take a step back, pump the brakes, and insert some distance between us.

It's what I usually do. Since I escaped Matt and started college, I've yet to have a relationship last longer than a few months, turning my back and walking away at the first sign of trouble.

But as much as I feel like an idiot for allowing myself to be vulnerable, every cell in my body says that I need to talk to him before making any decisions. Only, that's kind of hard to do when he won't answer his phone or return my texts.

My jaw clenches so fiercely as I end the call that my neck goes into spasm. My throat is so tight I can barely swallow. The rest of me isn't faring much better. I think I made a mistake. The question is, how badly have I messed up?

Before I can change my mind, I place another call. Drum my fingers on the kitchen table while I listen to it ring. Exhale a huge sigh of relief when it's answered.

"Hey, girl."

"Hi, Mallory."

"Director Jacobson filled me in on what happened. They just aren't giving you a break down there, are they?"

"They don't appear to be, no."

"Well, I haven't found anything useful yet, but don't worry, I will."

"Thanks, Mal. But actually… I'm not calling about that. I need some advice."

"Uh-oh."

"Yeah."

"Hold on a sec. I better sit down for this." A moment later she says, "Okay. Lay it on me."

So I do. I tell her about Jake's odd behavior. The

secrets he's kept. Everything I had to find out from Julian and the way Jake reacted when I spoke to him about what I had learned. How he took off and now refuses to answer my calls and texts.

"What do you think?" I ask. "Did I screw up? Was I out of line?"

My gut twists when my questions are met with silence. Mallory's never without words. The fact that she is now? It feels like all the confirmation I need. Finally, after what seems like years have passed, her voice carries over the line.

"Well, I mean, maybe? This Julian? He's the one Jake works with, right? The other senior partner?"

"Yes. Why?"

"Because I've seen his picture and, girl, he's hot. Not Jake hot, but a close enough second where he wouldn't feel like a consolation prize."

"But I have absolutely zero interest in him."

"I'm not sure that matters."

"There's no way that Jake would think that I was. That that's what this is about."

"Unless maybe you gave him a reason to," Mallory says gently. "Like believing the other man's word over his."

My acid reflux flares so bad it feels like I'm breathing fire. Like I'm melting from the inside. And I suspect that I might just deserve to.

The indignant anger I've been nursing between my pangs of regret since he walked out last night is suddenly gone, the coals now colder than if they'd been encased inside a glacier.

I deserve his silent treatment.

"I should grovel until he listens to my apology, shouldn't I?"

"I mean, I'm not going to tell you what to do. You do you, girl, but if it was me, I might just go ahead and bite the bullet and do it. What's it going to hurt, besides maybe your pride?"

The truth is, it won't even hurt that. Especially not if it brings Jake home.

"Any suggestions for how to do that when he won't talk to me?"

"I've heard showing up wearing nothing but an overcoat works."

Even though I would have thought it impossible given how miserable I feel right now, I laugh.

"Thanks, Mal."

"Don't mention it. And, Cassidy?"

"Yeah?"

"Don't worry. You guys will get through this."

"Yeah."

I wish I had her confidence about that, but I don't. I'm worried that I might have irreparably damaged our relationship. Broken Jake's trust. Driven a wedge between us that we'll never be able to remove. And if that's true, I don't know how I'll ever be able to forgive myself.

It's not only that without Jake I'm in this mess all alone. It's that without him, what's the point of fighting so hard to get out of it?

CHAPTER 18

I feel heavy, weighed down with remorse. Nausea coats my tongue with the thick fuzz of regret. I can't focus. I can't hold still. I can barely even breathe.

Jake still hasn't responded to any of my calls or texts, and I can't help thinking that maybe he *can't* answer. That maybe something bad happened when he left last night and I'll be forced to spend the rest of my life knowing that it's all my fault. That the last words between us were angry ones.

I'm making myself ill over it. I know I can't keep obsessing like this. I need to get away from this place, where everywhere I look I'm surrounded by memories that include Jake.

Carrying the raccoon back to her cage in the medical ward, I put her inside. The noise she makes as I close the door is enough to shred my already shattered heart into microscopic pieces. My molars grit even harder together as I rush from the room, practically jogging down the hall and out of the house.

Opening my car door, I feel my pocket before climbing inside, making sure I have the list of supplies I need to order from the feed store just outside of town. It's a task that Jake usually handles, but I'm not sure if I can rely on him to do it anymore.

I don't know what the future holds, but I do know that the animals need to eat. As much as I'm trying to hold on to my hope that Jake will forgive me, it's not fair to let them suffer for any reason, but especially not because I'm an idiot.

Reaching over, I turn the radio up a little louder, trying to drown out my thoughts. Scan the stations until I find one playing a song I used to love when I was in high school. Now it just sounds like noise. It's an odd form of torture, one that blessedly does the trick as I find myself pulling into the Gator Glade Feed and Seed lot and parking beside the large step van they use for deliveries.

A bell tinkles as I enter the store. Walking over to the counter, I pull my list from my pocket and wait. After a couple of minutes, my impatience grows. It's quickly replaced by worry.

Usually the owner, Donna, is perched on the stool behind the register. I've only seen her leave it when she's showing a customer where to find something, which takes a lot less time than I've been waiting. An itchy feeling takes hold as a memory of the robbery at the pharmacy rises to the surface of my mind.

As I take my first few hesitant steps toward the rear of the building, my hand instinctively moves behind my back, pulling the hem of my T-shirt up and tucking it inside my waistband so it's easier to access my concealed carry weapon. I keep my eyes wide, scanning my surroundings, looking for anything out of place as I creep down an aisle.

I've almost reached the back of the store when a murmured voice reaches my ears, the emotion in it causing the hair on my arms to rise. It's Donna's. And it sounds like she's crying.

Without hesitation I draw my pistol, quickening my steps until I reach the end of the row. Keeping the firearm concealed alongside my leg, I take a deep breath and step into the passage at the back of the store. Realize that my day just got infinitely worse as I quickly reholster the weapon.

"What's going on?" I ask as I hurry to Donna's side. "Is everything okay?"

"Yes." Sheriff Kingston responds with a single, sharp bark, his eyes narrowing.

At the same time, Donna turns her reddened eyes and puffy, tear-streaked face toward me and says, "No." Her hands grasp my arm in an iron grip, her voice hitching and high-pitched. "My granddaughter's gone missing."

"Oh, Donna," I say, my heart twisting into knots at the thought of what she's going through. "I'm so sorry. What can I do?"

"Now don't going telling her your business," Kingston warns. "This doesn't involve her." The sheriff points at me. "You remember that conversation we had the other day, don't you?"

"I do."

"Well, this is what I was talking about."

"Calm down, Lyle," Donna says. "She just wants to help."

"Trust me, you don't need her kind of help."

"Are you sure about that? Because you don't seem to be doing very much to find my granddaughter."

"Donna, I'm warning you. I won't be held responsible for anything that happens because that girl interferes with my investigation."

"*That girl* is an almost forty-year-old grown woman who's spent the last decade and a half as an FBI agent," I remind him.

Donna's eyes widen at my words. Her fingers tighten on me until it feels like she's crushing the bones beneath. "You're an FBI agent?"

I nod, suddenly regretting not keeping a better hold on my temper and outing myself.

"I didn't know."

"I…" My teeth dig at my lip, finding the tender raw spot I've made from chewing on it. Though I've been trying to keep my affiliation with the Bureau on a need-to-know basis since my return, this woman has helped me in every way she's been able, no questions asked. I should have confided in her, told her the truth before now. I promise myself I'll make it up to her.

"Not many people do. I'm on medical leave at the moment," I explain. "And the truth is, even once I'm cleared to return to active duty, I'm not sure I'm going to."

Ignoring the scoffing noise the sheriff makes, she says, "But still. You have experience with this kind of thing, right?"

"Not with missing teenagers, but with investigating in general, yes."

"You have to help, then. Please."

"Of course I will," I assure her. "I'll do whatever I can."

Sheriff Kingston curses. Donna shoots him a nasty look before continuing.

"My sixteen-year-old granddaughter and her friend

went hiking Monday. They never came home."

"Do you know where they went?"

She nods.

"Did you check the trailhead?" I ask Kingston.

"That's none of your concern," he answers.

"This doesn't have to be a pissing contest, Lyle. I'm just asking a question."

"And I'm just—"

"Yes!" Donna interrupts. "At least, he said he did."

The sheriff heaves the loudest sigh I've ever heard. "I assure you, one of my deputies was out there this morning. He said there were no cars in the lot."

"Did he check the trail log?" I ask.

Kingston's expression indicates that he has no idea what I'm talking about. He turns, angling his back to me.

"Donna, the two of us, we go way back. Longer than this one's even been alive. You need to trust me. I know it's hard to accept, but girls that age do these types of things. They get an idea in their head that they'll be better off on their own and decide to take off. As soon as they're out of money, they'll come home."

"And what if they don't?" I ask. "What if something bad happens to them first?"

"Now don't go making—"

"They didn't run away," Donna insists. "They wouldn't. You believe me, don't you, Cassidy?"

Before I can answer, the radio on Sheriff Kingston's shoulder crackles to life. Reaching for the device, he says, "Donna, you know I feel for you, I really do, but I've got a whole town to keep under control here. The girls will turn up. You need to believe me on this."

He starts backing away, toward the door. "And you," he points at me again, like I'm a dog he's commanding. "You need to remember that you don't have jurisdiction in my town."

The finger stays aimed in my direction until he's no longer in sight. A moment later, the bell on the door rings, celebrating his exit.

I fight the urge to chase after him. Taking a deep breath, my fingers unfurl from the fists they've formed. Putting a palm on Donna's shoulder, I give her what I hope is an encouraging smile.

"I believe you," I assure her. "Which trail did they go hiking at?"

"The Indigo Hammock."

It feels like a boulder just dropped in my stomach. "And you said they were out there Monday?"

"Yes."

I swallow hard, but my throat's too tight for anything to get past. It doesn't matter, because my mouth has gone dryer than an empty frying pan left on a hot burner too long.

"Are their names Amelia Owens and Danielle Fuller?"

Donna's lips tremble as she asks, "How'd you know that?"

"Because I was out there on Monday searching for that raccoon you called me about. And those were the two names that had signed in on the trail log ahead of me."

But they hadn't signed out by the time I left. And there'd been no other vehicles in the parking lot.

"So that means they were there, right?" she asks, a ray of hope brightening her eyes.

"Yes, I believe it does."

What I don't believe is that two sixteen-year-old girls went hiking before they decided to run away. Or that they went through the hassle of driving all the way out there to sign the log just to throw off anyone looking for them. Which means that sometime that day, they ran into trouble. The question is, was it on the trail, or on the way home?

"Then where are they now?"

"I don't know," I say. "But I'm going to do my best to find out. I'll stop by the house and grab some gear, then hit the trail. I'll let you know what I find."

Donna's entire body seems to deflate as she utters a tearful, "Thank you."

Hurrying from the store, I groan as I calculate the time since they went missing. No doubt Kingston waited until he absolutely had to before starting an investigation. What was it he said? That one of his deputies had checked out there this morning?

Which means no one checked the trail for signs of a struggle before yesterday's rain. Any drag marks or blood would most likely have washed away. And though I was out there the day they went missing, I was looking for an arrow made of branches and a raccoon. Big picture, not tiny details.

Passing my car, I walk to the far side of the step van I parked next to, checking to see if Sheriff Kingston's cruiser is there. It's not.

I'm not sure whether to be disappointed or relieved that the man has left. If he'd had only a bit more patience, or interest in helping, he'd have still been here for this development. And I know better than to approach him for an assist. Which means I'll just have to hope that whatever I find, it's something that I can handle on my own.

CHAPTER 19

I flinch as the shadow swoops toward me. Tell myself to relax when I realize it's just a bird. But no matter how many times I tell myself there's nothing to fear, my body remains tied in knots. Because the truth is, there's plenty to be afraid of.

The world is a dangerous place. I know this more than most. And I know the statistics that back it up. I try not to think of them now as I make my way deeper into the woods.

Before I left the sanctuary, I took the time to feed and water everyone, suspecting I'd be home late. Though it's already early afternoon, it stays light until nine this time of year. I intend to search for those girls every second I can. If that means walking back in the dark, so be it. It's not like I have anything to go home to.

Though I'd called Jake before I left the shelter of my car at the trailhead, he once again failed to answer, sending me to voicemail after two rings. I hung up without leaving a message. He either wants to hear from me or he doesn't.

Clearly, he doesn't. There's no use forcing the issue.

My phone pings, filling me with a jolt of elation, hoping that I had the thought too soon. But when I pull it from my pocket and wake the screen, I find that it's not a text from Jake, like I'd foolishly hoped. It's not a text at all.

I hold my breath as I press the notification from the security camera mounted above the front door. The one that boasts *human image detected.* But it's not Jake who appears on the screen. It's Julian.

Groaning, I squint at the image. Pinch the screen and spread my fingers to enlarge it. Though the clip is in black and white, I'm fairly certain that the darkness encircling the man's right eye isn't a shadow. It's a bruise. And I only need one guess as to where he got it.

Cursing, I turn my screen off and tuck the phone back into my pocket. I don't have time for this drama right now. There are much more important things, two of which might be somewhere on this trail right now in need of help.

Quickening my pace, I scan my surroundings. Ancient oaks crowd the sides of trail, their heavy boughs, draped with Spanish moss, create a canopy above it. Saw palmettos and scrub litter the forest floor. Wild coffee scents the humid air. Narrow paths disappear into the brush, but none are big enough to accommodate a human.

Adjusting my pack, I continue on. Though I'm not quite as far in as I made it last time, when I found the raccoon, my back already aches twice as bad. The straps dig deep into my shoulders, weighted by the extra supplies I carry. My sun shirt is drenched with sweat, my hiking pants well on their way to being the same.

This time, my bag is packed so full I could hardly zip it. The first aid kit I'm carrying is over ten pounds just by itself. Add in the rope, paracord, knife, water purifying tablets, emergency blankets, fire starters, ready meals, a solar phone charger, glowsticks, flares, a compass, a multitool, and enough bottled water to keep three people alive in this heat for a couple of days and it feels like I'm giving a piggyback ride to an NFL player.

But if there's one thing Butch taught me, it's that it's better to be overprepared than under. An image of his face pops into my mind, his expression equal parts patience and amusement, though I know that my own face, the one that matches this memory, is anything but.

Finally, we come to a stop. Butch wraps a hand around my arm, uses it to spin me around in circles. Then, he lifts the blindfold. I scowl as I look around at my surroundings.

When my grandfather promised me a break from the endless work at the sanctuary before school started, this wasn't what I had in mind. I thought he was going to take me shopping, or maybe even to a movie.

Instead, while the rest of the girls entering the freshman class with me are probably painting their nails and deciding how to wear their hair, I'm here, somewhere in the middle of the woods, with no trail in sight. Drenched in sweat, covered in a thick coat of grime that's probably going to make me break out for the first day of class, and being crushed under the weight of the pack strapped to my back.

I raise an eyebrow as I notice that Butch isn't carrying any supplies. Apparently, I've graduated from granddaughter to pack mule.

"How are you going to find your way back to the car?" he asks me.

"I'm going to follow you."

He shakes his head. "It's up to you to get us out of here. How are you going to do it?"

I sigh. Glare up at the sky, where the sun is to my left.

It was early when we set out. The day was still breaking, but when we left the car, the soft light chasing away the fading grey of dawn was to my right. Though we hiked for hours, it still has to be morning.

Pointing at the blinding brightness, I say, "We go that way. East."

Butch nods his approval. "Good. Now what is the most pressing need you're going to have to satisfy?"

"Getting this pack off my back, followed by emptying my bladder."

"Cassidy."

"Fine. Water."

"And how are you going to get it?"

"I'm guessing you mean other than grabbing a bottle out of the bag?"

"Yes."

"What can I use?"

"Anything in your pack other than the bottled water."

I grumble as I slide the rucksack off and squat beside it. Rummage around, then pull out the plastic grocery bag I keep in it to carry out any trash I make. I give Butch a look, aware that he's going to want a demonstration, so without waiting for instructions, I pick up a small, smooth rock and wipe it clean on my pants.

Placing the rock in the corner of the bag, I spin slowly in a circle until I spot a plant I recognize. Covering a patch of star grass with the bag, I loop one of the handles tightly around the opening. Turning back to Butch, I smirk and say, "Water vapor from plants."

"Why'd you choose that plant in particular?"

"Because I recognize it and know it's not toxic."

"Excellent. What would you do if you didn't recognize any of the plants?"

"Find some grass to lay the plastic out on."

That hadn't been the only time Butch took me out into the woods for survival training. By the time I graduated from high school, he could drop me off in the middle of nowhere and I could find my way back. Sometimes, he'd simulate injury situations, a broken femur, a head wound, and have me administer first aid before crafting a way to get the injured party back to safety.

Though at the time it had seemed unnecessary and excessive, I'm grateful for every second he spent training me now. Because if the missing girls are still out here, something happened to them. If one or both of them is hurt, they've been that way for days. Being able to administer proper care could mean the difference between life and death.

I remind myself of this each time I think about stashing some of my supplies to lighten the load, though there is one thing I can do to make myself more comfortable. As much as I've been fighting it, the time has come to empty my bladder. Apparently, my needs while hiking haven't changed much.

Slowing my pace, I start looking for a spot, searching for any little alcove off the trail. My hands wrap around the straps of my pack in anticipation of slipping it off, if only for a few minutes. They curl tighter as something catches my attention.

Coming to a stop in the middle of the path, I continue to stare. As I do, a ripple of unease spreads through me. My skin pricks uncomfortably, the hair on the back of my neck bristling as I take a step closer.

There, gathered in a heap, is a collection of branches. It's not something that could have happened naturally. In fact, as I tear my gaze away to look at the canopy above me, I note that there are none of a similar size overhead. They don't even belong to the same type of tree.

Someone purposely collected these sticks.

Remembering the arrow I'd been looking for the other day, I pull my phone out and check the time. This is about where I found the raccoon, which means this pile of branches was probably the landmark I was looking for. But someone had already shoved them to the side by the time I arrived.

Who? The girls? Or someone else?

There were no other names on the trail log Monday, but plenty of hikers don't bother signing in or out. And though there'd been no other vehicles in the lot, that doesn't mean there wasn't someone else out here that day. It also doesn't mean they aren't still out here now.

Suddenly, it makes sense. How tame the raccoon I rescued is. The bait trap she had stuck on her head despite being miles from civilization. Someone must be living out here in these woods.

A shudder runs through me as I wonder if that's why the girls never made it home. The sweat coating my skin turns icy as I consider what might have happened to them. My bladder twinges when I realize how silent it's fallen.

There's no bird song. No twigs snapping or leaves rustling under the weight of a squirrel. Even the breeze has fallen still. It's just me and the heavy sound of my breathing. And a sudden crash in the brush to my right.

I turn to face the noise, my movements slow and stilted under the weight of my pack. Realize my mistake a second too late. I spin toward the sound of heavy footsteps approaching from behind, but the impact of something hard against my skull stops me.

CHAPTER 20

I can't breathe. There's something heavy on my chest, weighing my lungs down. I try to reach for it, but my arms won't move. At the same time, I feel in motion, like the ground is bouncing beneath me. Or is it that I'm bouncing on the ground?

I tell my eyes to open and check, but they don't want to. It's too hard. My head pounds like it's been struck by a train. All I want to do is go back to sleep. Then something snags my hair and my lids part wider than I would have thought possible.

I snap my jaw shut before I can scream. Stare in horror at the hazy branches and leaves above me. I'm being dragged.

Quickly, I close my eyes all but a tiny sliver, but try as I might, I can't see the person who has my ankles locked in a vise-like grip. I can hear the wheeze of his breath, though, thick and phlegmy. His labored grunts as he struggles to pull me across the forest floor.

I dare to open the slits I'm watching through a little

wider. I still can't see who has me. I can, however, see my pack on top of my chest, my hands bound to it by the straps. At least it's one mystery solved.

Now I just have to figure out who my captor is. What he wants with me. How long I was unconscious. Where the two teenage girls I was looking for are, and how to get back to the main trail.

I assure myself it will be easy enough, but the fireworks going off inside my head disagree. The nausea I feel and the slight blur to my vision suggest that whatever was used to hit me left me with a concussion. It's not the first I've had, but I have a sickening feeling that I'm going to have one heck of a battle in front of me if I don't want it to be my last.

Finally, the world stops moving. I snap my eyes shut. Force my face slack. Resist the urge to try and wipe at the line of drool I feel leaking down the side of my cheek. It's not like I can reach it, anyway.

But the sensation it creates is unnerving. Even though I know what it is, it feels like an insect crawling across my skin. I might sell my soul to get it to stop. Only, then I'm moving again and I find I have bigger worries as the ground beneath me changes from dirt and leaves and rocks and sticks to a wood plank floor.

The brightness filtering through my eyelids dims. The air turns stale, thick with the stench of body odor and trash. And the soft whimpers I hear suggest that I'm not the only one here in this place who's scared.

My heels are set on the floor with surprising gentleness. The thud of heavy steps approaches my head, then passes it. There's the click of a door shutting. Though I still hear the whimpers, I no longer hear the labored breathing. Even so, I continue to keep my eyes shut, to feign unconsciousness.

I struggle not to react as a loud buzz comes from outside, a motor of some sort. The sound grows fainter, fading into the distance. After what feels like a century has passed, I dare to take a look at my surroundings.

The wooden walls are rough, the floor even rougher, dirt embedded deep into the texture of the planks. Light filters in through a small window smeared with grease and grime. A small propane camp stove rests to my right. And to my left, huddled together on a filthy sleeping bag, are two teenage girls.

"Amelia?" My voice sounds raspy and hoarse. I have to dig deep to speak loud enough to be heard. "Danielle?"

They exchange a startled look, holding an entire silent conversation about me with their eyes.

"I'm a friend of your grandmother's." Realizing I don't know which of the girls is Donna's granddaughter, I add, "From the feed store."

"Gran?" The smaller of the two girls begins to cry. Her companion tries to comfort her, but I realize that I haven't seen their hands. They must be bound.

"What are you tied to?" I ask, wiggling my own fingers. Lancing pain replaces the numbness as blood flows back into them.

"There are knotholes in the wall. The ropes are through them," the larger girl, a brunette, says.

"Are the edges sharp?"

"Not sharp enough to cut through the rope. We tried that already."

Crap. That means I need to get free before the man returns.

"How long do you think we have until he comes back?" I ask. Squirming under the weight of my pack, trying to make enough slack in the straps to get my hands out, I realize my pockets are empty. That means no car keys, no phone.

I round my lower back against the floor. No gun. The acrid taste of fear makes my mouth pucker.

"He took the bike. He's usually gone a while when he does that."

I imagine him racing to the trailhead to move my car. The same way he must have after he snatched the girls.

"He's not as bad as the other one," the smaller girl says.

"The other one? There's two of them?" I ask.

"Yeah." The brunette's voice trembles as she adds, "He's the one we worry might kill us."

The blood in my veins turns to ice, making my struggle against the straps binding me even clumsier. I stop a moment. Close my eyes. Draw several deep breaths while I give myself a silent pep talk. Then I renew my efforts, fighting even harder against my bonds.

Because if I don't get free, neither do these girls.

"We're going to get out of here," I say, as much for myself as for them. "All of us."

I remind myself that there's two men I have to watch out for. Two men, two girls, and one me, weakened and with a headache to end all headaches. I'm not sure I can walk, much less run.

But maybe I won't need to.

"How well do you know these woods?" I ask.

"Pretty good," the brunette says. "I've been coming out here with my family since I was little."

"Were you conscious when you were brought here?"

"Yes."

"How do we get back to the main trail?"

"It's to the east."

"You sure?"

"Yes."

"Can you girls climb?"

"What, you mean like a tree?"

"Yes."

This time, when they exchange looks, I see something besides fear in their eyes.

"You better believe it."

"Good. Because if one or both of the men are here when we get our chance, I want you to run away from the path, behind the cabin, and climb the first tree you can. Separate trees, so you won't have to wait for each other. Can you do that?"

"What about you?"

"Don't wait for me. If they're here, I'm going to have to keep them busy long enough for you to have enough of a head start that you'll be in your trees before they start looking for you. We need them to not realize they're searching in the wrong direction."

"Then what?"

"Wait until they give up and stop looking. Once they're back inside, climb down and hike out of here. Once you hit the trail, run. He moved your car, probably mine too, so you'll have to head back to town on foot. Stay near the wood line so you can hide if you hear his bike."

"You're talking like you won't be with us."

I shrug. "I might not. If that's the case, try and remember how to get back here so you can send help. Can you do that?" When they don't respond, I add, "We might only get one chance. Can I trust you to take it?"

"Yes," the smaller girl says.

The brunette promises, "You can."

I give them what I hope is a reassuring smile as I

continue to work my wrists free from the straps. Because I know that talking about it is the easy part. The hard part is surviving it.

CHAPTER 21

I am not all right. My head feels like someone stabbed a hot poker through my eye and used it to stir around. My movements are slow, my limbs heavy, my thoughts scattered. And yet, I have to keep going.

Freeing my hands took longer than I'd hoped. After my wrists had been thoroughly twisted through the straps of my pack, my captor, whoever he is, had used the excess to tie multiple knots, further complicating my escape.

And though I wish I could say that I'd hit the ground running once I'd gotten loose, that would be a lie. I couldn't even sit up, the weight of the bag on my chest too heavy for me in my weakened state. Finally, I managed to tip it off by rolling onto my side. Even then, functioning was a struggle.

My hands shook as I unzipped the pack and rooted around until I found the small pocketknife stashed inside. My entire body trembled as I half crawled, half dragged myself over to the girls. My muscles burned with fatigue as I used the blade to saw through the rope binding them. Though it wasn't that thick, he'd tied a number of knots, same as he'd done to me.

Between my addled state and the waning light inside the shack, it was hard to determine where I needed to cut. What's worse, once I finally did get through the rope, we discovered that it only freed one hand of each girl. There was a second strand still looped through the knothole, holding them hostage.

Fortunately, they've been taking turns attacking the tie that still binds them with the ever-dulling knife blade. Eighty percent of the fiber is now severed. In another ten minutes or so, they'll be free.

The brunette, Danielle, chugs from the bottle of water I gave her while the smaller girl, Donna's granddaughter, Amelia, continues sawing at the rope. A small bubble of hope forms inside me as I watch the strand get thinner and thinner. It vanishes an instant later, popped by the buzzing sound of an approaching motor.

All three of us curse. Amelia works harder, her motions growing more frantic as I gather our bottles and shove them back into the pack.

"Keep working," I say, turning toward the door. Though I briefly consider trying to lock him out somehow, I know it's useless. He might have a key. Whatever he used to hit me could easily break the window. Not to mention that he has my gun.

Which is why trying to take him by surprise also isn't an option. If I was at full strength, I'd risk it. I'd take that tiny pocketknife and plunge it as deep as I could into his eye, or his throat, or whatever vulnerable spot I could reach. But in my current condition I might not cause more than a flesh wound. I can't risk it, not when it's not just myself I'd be putting in jeopardy.

The noise has grown louder, so close now that I can feel it in my joints. He's almost here. Slowly, I lower myself onto the floor.

"Turn around like you were when I got here," I tell the girls. "Pretend like your hands are still bound. Don't let him see you messing with the rope, but whenever he's not looking, keep trying to get free. I'll do my best to distract him."

Their faces fill with terror as I lie down on my side. Wrapping both arms around the pack, I roll over onto my back, lifting the bag on top of my chest again. The effort causes a fresh wave of pain to jolt through me, sending me into a sweat.

Whispering, I say, "Once you're free, I need you to let me know. I want one of you to ask: is that a raccoon?"

I fight tears as I loop my arms back through the straps. As the engine stops. As I force my eyes to shut.

It feels like I've been shoved deep underwater as the door opens, my body not allowing my lungs to fill, my ears popping from the pressure. A large shadow falls over me, bringing the sound of heavy breathing closer. I flinch as the heat of that breath hits my cheek, the stench of it reaching my nose.

I flutter my eyes open, pretending like I'm just waking for the first time. But what I don't have to fake is the fear caused by the face that fills my vision.

For a moment I wonder if I'm hallucinating. Maybe this whole ordeal has been nothing but a bad dream. Because the skin-covered skull leaning over me, his crusting sores oozing puss, is straight out of a nightmare.

"Oh, good." The man sighs as he straightens, scratching at a scab on his arm. Doesn't seem to notice when it starts bleeding. "I was afraid I hit you too hard. I tried to bunt"—he mimics the action with his other hand, a wooden baseball bat clenched in his filthy fingers—"but you turned at the last minute."

I act like I'm trying to feel the injury on my scalp, struggling against the straps like they're still tight enough to hold me.

"Who are you? Why'd you hit me?" I ask.

"I—I had to."

"Why?"

"Because you were looking for me. You wanted to turn me in."

The man is clearly an addict. If I had to wager a guess, I'd say meth. The sores that cover him are common among methamphetamine users. As is his paranoia. And though his accusation isn't entirely wrong, I intend to use his muddled mental state to my advantage.

"I don't even know who you are," I say.

"Then why were you out here?"

"I was hiking."

"With this?" The girls gasp as he pulls my firearm out and waves it around. "If that's true, why'd you have a gun?"

"For protection. Not that it did me any good."

His yellowed eyes dart between me and the girls. I act like I just noticed them.

"Who are they? Where'd you get them?"

"They were trying to turn me in too. They made a big arrow so the cops would know where to find me."

No wonder I never found the marker made by the woman who reported the raccoon. This man, in his paranoid state, thought that it had something to do with him. And that's why he took the girls. I swallow a lump of guilt.

"They're children," I say.

He squints into the shadows where they huddle, taking a closer look. "No."

"They can't be more than sixteen."

"Um."

"Do you need help?"

"What?"

The question seems to take him by surprise. That's what I need to do—keep him off balance and disoriented.

Softening my expression, I say, "You seem like a really nice guy."

He nods.

"If you're in some kind of trouble, maybe I can help."

He sinks to the floor beside me. I need to get him to turn his back to the girls so they can keep working to free themselves.

"How?"

"Can you help me sit up?"

He gives me a wary look but shifts his weight so he can grab the pack. As he lifts it, pulling me into a sitting position, I stretch my fingers until they're lightly touching his arm. Repulsion rises inside me at the feel of his clammy skin against mine, but I do my best to ignore it.

Forcing a smile, I say, "Thank you. I appreciate your kindness."

I refuse to glance at the girls. I can't risk drawing attention to them—I'll just have to hope that they're using the opportunity to work on freeing themselves the rest of the way.

"What's your name?" I ask.

"They call me Worm."

He looks like a worm. Painfully skinny, his body lax in a way that suggests he's boneless, flesh slightly sticky to the touch. I tighten my muscles, bracing myself, resisting a shudder.

"I'm Cassidy. Why are you out here, Worm?"

"What do you mean?"

"Is this where you live?"

"Why do you want to know?"

He draws away, breaking the connection between my fingertips and his forearm. Scoots backward, putting distance between us as he stares at me suspiciously. I've messed up. Triggered his paranoia. But as a buzz sounds in the distance, that suspicion morphs into something else.

One of the girls whimpers and I realize what that something is—fear.

It seems I'm about to meet the other man who calls this rundown shack home, and judging from everyone's reactions, that's a very bad thing.

CHAPTER 22

The odds just got worse. Any minute now, one opponent will become two. Two men who have their freedom, my firearm, and probably not a lot to lose, whereas I have a throbbing headache that's growing worse by the second. Hindered reaction times. Two terrified girls and endless miles to cover to get back to civilization. I have to try and gain the upper hand before things get any worse.

"I could take the girls. Get them back home. Return them to their parents." I speak quickly, knowing that I'm running out of time.

"No way. You'd tell the police. Show them where to find me."

"That's not true. None of us want to hurt you or get you in trouble. We could leave and it would be like we were never even here. Isn't that right, girls?"

"Yes."

"She's right."

His eyes yoyo between me and the door as the noise outside grows louder.

"Please. I can tell you're a good guy. I know you don't want to see anyone get hurt."

His Adam's apple bobs, the knobby bone thrusting against the skin of his throat as he swallows hard.

"You could come with us, if you'd like. I don't have much, just a small home, but you could live there with me. I could take care of you."

The engine falls silent.

"Really?"

"Really." I give him the best smile I can muster.

"Why would you do that?"

"Because I… I'm lonely. And it's nice to have someone to share things with. Don't you think?"

My heart hammers so hard that my chest feels bruised by it. Each surge of blood it sends into my veins makes the pounding in my head worse. The pain is overwhelming, the dizziness so bad that I worry I might pass out.

But I need to find a way to get the girls out of here, first. Whatever it takes.

"Maybe."

I stretch my fingers toward him again. Wiggle them with a hopeful look, praying he'll reach out and take them. But as the sound of steps approaches the door behind me, and he scoots farther away from me across the floor, I know I've lost the battle.

"What's going on here?"

Danielle whimpers. Fresh tears cut tracks through the dirt on Amelia's face. Both of them shrink back, pressing themselves against the wall.

"Worm?"

"I… I had to. She was going to find us and turn us in."

The man behind me curses. There's something

familiar about it.

"Your brain's fried, you know that?"

"I'm sorry, Skunk. Really."

"You should be. I told you to take care of the other two while I was gone. Instead, you went and made it worse."

"I didn't mean to." Worm gets to his feet, wringing his hands. "Did I really make it worse?"

"Yes!" the other man snarls. "I swear, you're the dumbest—I mean, what were you even thinking?"

I shoot a quick glance at the girls. Amelia's eyes look over my head at the arguing men as she mouths *almost*.

Slowly, I start unraveling my wrists from the pack straps.

"What are we supposed to do with them?"

"Maybe they could take care of us?" Worm offers hopefully.

"Maybe they could take care of us," Skunk mocks in a falsetto.

Then, in a much deeper voice, one that makes my skin tighten on my bones and sends a fresh surge of adrenaline into my veins, he growls, "Where'd you get that gun?"

"She had it."

I force my face into the most pitiful expression I can muster. It doesn't take much work.

"Who, her? Hey, new girl."

I turn my head slowly until I'm looking over my shoulder. The last shred of hope I'd been holding onto vanishes instantly.

"You!"

The hand strikes out faster than my addled brain can follow. I yelp as I'm yanked to my feet, my shoulder feeling like it just tore from its socket as gravity and the weight of my pack jerk it in the other direction. I manage to catch it before it drops and reveals that my hands aren't bound anymore, though the fingers digging deep into my muscles makes it hard to hold on.

"You know her?" Worm's voice is pure disbelief.

"That's the chick who screwed me up at the pharmacy. If it wasn't for her, I'd have got the stuff to give to Dave for him to cook us up a batch." He glares at me in a way that makes my breath catch as he says, "She's the reason why you're feeling so bad right now, man. And why you're tearing yourself to shreds. That's gross. Stop it."

Reaching out, he smacks Worm's hand as he digs at a sore on his arm.

"What's she doing out here?"

"That's a very good question."

The man called Skunk snatches my gun from Worm's hand. He racks the slide. The round that was already chambered ejects. But I know that the moment he released it, another moved to take its place, which makes it that much harder for me to maintain my courage as he shoves the barrel against my forehead.

"And you better have a very good answer," he threatens me.

I straighten my spine. Lift my chin. Force the fear from my eyes as I meet his gaze.

"Is that a raccoon?"

"Ricky!" Worm's head whips around as he looks for the animal.

Skunk's focus shifts for only an instant, but it's all I need. I swing my arms, hitting his gun hand with the full weight of my pack. The weapon fires, splinters spraying from a hole near the ceiling as I yell to the girls, "Run!"

Lowering my shoulder, I ram it into the man, using my momentum to slam him into the wall as I reach for the firearm with both hands. But my coordination is off, my movements too slow. His elbow catches me in the temple, right in the fluid-filled bruise left by the baseball bat.

I collapse to the floor like a puppet with its strings cut. My vision goes in and out of focus. In, Worm staring at me in horror, his hands curled into fists against his mouth. Out, darkness. In, the sleeping bag where the girls had been, now empty. Out, darkness. In, a fist, letters I can't read tattooed below each knuckle zooming toward my face. Then there's nothing but the darkness.

CHAPTER 23

My pulse *whooshes* like a fetal monitor in my ears. The sound of it's too loud, the force of it too hard. I shift, trying to alleviate the pressure, but everything hurts—my face, my head, my body… my heart. Even my thoughts.

I pray that the girls make it home safe because I'm really starting to doubt that a similar destiny is in my future. If it isn't, I wonder how Jake will handle my loss.

It seems a silly thing to worry about as I lie here with the acrid taste of copper sharp in my mouth, the side of my face sticky with blood. Wincing as the floorboards tremble beneath my skull as Skunk paces the tiny room, waving a gun—my gun—around, making threats.

I peel one of my eyes open a slit to see who he's talking to, but besides the two of us, no one's here. I'm not sure how long I was unconscious. Or what I plan to do now that I'm not. I know I need to try and escape, but how? I suppose getting up would be a start.

I try to push myself up but can't. My hands are

bound. My whole body is, a length of rope coiled around me from my armpits to my ankles. The discovery takes the last little shred of hope I'd been holding on to and pulverizes it.

How can I get out of here if I can't fight?

Heavy steps approach from outside. I'm not sure whether to pray for a miracle or yell for whoever it is to run as Skunk spins to face it, aiming my gun at the gap as it slowly opens. Worm appears at the threshold, a hangdog expression drawing his narrow face down, creating folds he's far too young to have.

He lifts timid eyes as he admits, "I couldn't find them."

An angry roar fills the room. A bottle smashes against the wall, shards of glass flying across the shack, some of them pelting me as they land. I sneak a glance at the men, checking to see if either of them has realized I'm awake. They haven't.

I roll slightly, tipping the debris off myself. Even that small movement causes a swell of nausea to rise inside me. I hold my breath as I fight it back, afraid that even the simple act of filling my lungs might be too much motion for me right now.

If I wasn't concussed before, I know that I am now. But that's okay. I can still do this. I just need to stay sharp.

And speaking of sharp… I stare at the chunk of glass on the floor beside me, trying to figure out how to get my hands on it. It's only six inches away, but given the way I feel, it might as well be a mile.

"What do you mean you couldn't find them?" Skunk shouts. "Where'd you look?"

"Everywhere."

"Like? Tell me."

"I ran all the way to the main trail, but I didn't see a thing. Didn't hear anything, either. So I doubled back, looped around the cabin a few times, searched all the brush, but there was no sign of them."

I chance a small, shallow breath, feeling relieved. The girls must have climbed like I told them to.

"You."

A worn pair of sneakers appears in front of my face. I try not to react and reveal that I'm conscious again but can't help flinching when one of the shoes comes toward my face, the toe of it jabbing my forehead roughly.

"Where would they go?"

I swallow hard, trying to keep the balloon that I feel floating up my throat down.

The shoe shoves me again as Skunk yells, "Where?"

"I don't know."

"Bull."

"I only met them today."

Turning to Worm, he points at me. "Get her up."

Worm looks at me nervously. "Why?"

"Because I told you to."

The thin man moves behind me. A moment later, I feel his hands tucking into my armpits. He tries to lift me gently, but even so, the motion is too much. That balloon I've been fighting? Any second now it's going to pop.

"You're taking too long."

Skunk grabs a handful of the rope that binds me and yanks me up. The world tilts. My body lurches. The bubble inside me bursts. A hot stream of vomit erupts from me, hitting the floor with a splash.

"Sick."

Skunk gives me a shove as he releases me. I use the momentum to aim my fall, landing on my side next to the glass. Stretch my fingers, trying to reach it, but it's still too far away from my hand.

I grunt as Skunk uses his foot to roll me onto my back. "You're going to clean that up."

"Yes," I say, hoping he'll cut my hands free so I can do it.

"This whole thing is your fault." The glare he gives me is toxic. I shift my gaze from his face to my firearm, aimed at my head, wondering if this is it. "You're nothing but trouble."

His gun hand moves. I squeeze my eyes shut. Try to conjure up an image of Jake's face, Butch's smile, Stephano's dancing, memories from a life that still feels so horribly incomplete.

The crack of the shot echoes in the small room. I feel the force of it in my bones. The heat of the blood as it spatters across me, dampening my clothes. But what I don't feel is where I've been hit.

I push my eyes open. They land on a cartoon of a half-naked woman riding a shark. It's the back of Skunk's shirt. The man isn't even facing my direction.

Was he just trying to scare me? No. Because as I continue to look around, I see the victim of his anger lying on the floor by my legs. It's Worm. And there's a bullet hole right where his nose used to be.

Skunk turns slowly. This time, when our gazes meet, there's a smile stretched across his face.

"That's one problem down." He uses the barrel of the gun to point at me. "Now one more to go."

"You don't want to do that," I rush to say.

His smile vanishes. "Give me one good reason why I shouldn't."

I'm desperate. I only have one trick up my sleeve, and it isn't even really a trick. It might not even work, and if it does, it's just delaying the inevitable. But maybe, if I buy myself enough time, I'll find a way out of this.

"My name is Cassidy Knox," I say. "I'm the one responsible for putting Tony Bianchi in prison. Do you know who he is?"

Skunk's eyes widen. He licks his lips as he stares at me. "Yeah. I've heard of Tony."

"He wants revenge. Put a bounty on my head to get it. Which means that I'm worth far more to you alive than dead."

"How much?"

"I don't know. If you were him, how much do you think you'd pay to get your hands on the woman who took away your freedom?"

His mouth twists into a knot. His foot starts tapping rapidly against the floor.

"How do I know you're telling the truth?"

"You won't until you check. Do you know anyone with ties to him? Who could get him a message, maybe?"

"Yeah."

"Why don't you call them?"

"He's not the kind of guy you call. I'm gonna have to go see him in person."

Skunk crosses to the door, giving me a threatening look.

"If this is some kind of trick…"

"It's not," I assure him.

"It better not be. 'Cause if it is, you'll regret it when I get back. I'll make sure of it."

With that, he steps outside. I breathe a sigh of relief, almost unable to believe my luck. He's gone. I hope the girls have gotten enough of a head start that they'll be able to hide when they hear his bike coming.

As for me… I turn my focus to the piece of glass on

the floor before me. It's the same size and shape as a tortilla chip, but with a much sharper edge. And if I can just get my hands on it, I know I'll be able to get free.

Rolling onto my side with a groan, I buck my hips forward, tightening my muscles, dragging myself closer to it. The action sends electric jolts of agony through my skull, causing me to break out in a sweat. Tears squeeze from my eyes, and my breath becomes a ragged pant. All that for one, maybe two inches of movement. But every centimeter brings me closer to freedom.

A noise behind me causes me to fall still. My heart feels like it just skipped a beat. Maybe I won't have to put forth the effort. Maybe the girls are still here and now they're coming for me.

I stare at the door expectantly. But it's not Amelia or Danielle who appears.

Skunk circles behind me, grabs me by the arms and drags me over to the sleeping bag the girls were on when I first arrived. The ragged ends of the rope we cut through stick through the knotholes again. He uses them to tie me to the wall.

This time, when he leaves, there is no hope. There's just me, unable to move. Looking at the shard of glass across the room until darkness falls and I can no longer see it. Suspecting that I just traded a quick death for a far more painful one.

CHAPTER 24

Every time I open my eyes, all that's changed is the shadows. I have no idea how much time has passed, whether it's been hours or days. I know only that the ache in my head has finally started to fade—but I'm not sure if that's a good thing.

Because all of my senses have started to dull. I can no longer smell the metallic odor of Worm's blood or my own. The sound of the wind ruffling through the trees and the birdsong I know must still surround the shack have been replaced by the gentle lull of the ocean in my ears.

The objects that share the room with me have lost their distinct edges and are now surrounded by hazy halos. My skin is numb and my limbs feel foreign, like they belong to a different body. My hands are squeezed shut, too weak and cramped to work. Even the hard knot of hunger that's plagued me has faded. The only thing that remains sharp is the bite of my thirst.

My mouth is a desert, my tongue rough and cracked,

my throat clenched tight like a fist. Even my teeth, when I try to suck them to work up some spit, are painfully dry.

I don't know which of my symptoms have been caused by my concussion and which are the result of dehydration. I don't have the energy to care. Every time my thoughts start to drift to the hopelessness of my situation, I pray for sleep. And blessedly, it comes.

Which is why I'm not sure if I'm dreaming or not when Skunk appears before me. Not until he cuts me free from the wall. With nothing holding me upright, I slump over, falling onto my side.

He stands over me, his mouth moving. He gestures with his hands. Frowns.

I close my eyes and wait for sleep to come back and claim me once more.

But then I'm moving. He grunts as he drags me by my ankles. Across the room. Out the door. Over sticks and leaves and dirt until he finally releases me next to a cart attached to a rusting motorized bike.

He isn't gentle as he wrestles me into it, my bonds straining as he forces my body to contort. The heat, as he covers me with a tarp, is almost unbearable. The inch of water I'm resting in feels like it's boiling. I turn my head and drink it anyway. Push a leaf out of my mouth with my tongue. And slowly feel myself reanimate.

I'm careful as I unclench my left fist. The one with the small pocketknife grasped inside. The pocketknife that the girls left behind when they escaped.

I hadn't been able to open it. I'd spent hours trying, but my coordination had been too clumsy to hook a nail into the small crescent on the edge. But now, I try again.

I'm fueled by desperation. Sheer stubbornness. And, when the intense pain returns to my head as I'm bounced and jarred over the rough forest floor, fury. I'm not going down without a fight.

I have no idea what that fight is going to look like yet, only that it's not going to be pretty. Because as I manage to pull the blade from its housing, get it under the rope by my wrist and start sawing, all I can think about is how it's going to feel when I jam the dull piece of metal into Skunk's body—preferably in time to get away before he turns me over to Bianchi's men.

It's that desire that keeps me working long after the water is gone and my clothes are drenched in sweat. As the uneven terrain turns into the smooth surface of road. And as my bonds ever so slowly begin to fray and loosen.

The drone of the engine drops in pitch as we slow. The bike turns but fails to regain speed, inching along until we come to a stop. The motor ceases. In the sudden silence, I hear Skunk's feet as he dismounts and they hit the ground.

I'm out of time. A blanket of panic wraps tight around me. My heart beats erratically. Reluctantly, I remove the knife from beneath the rope and slide it up under the sleeve of my sun shirt, holding it in place with my thumb.

The tarp above me is snatched away. I suck in giant lungful's of fresh air, wincing against the blinding sunlight. Struggle to maintain my grip on my weapon as I'm rolled over the side of the cart onto the hard, unforgiving asphalt.

Skunk's hands wrap around me, digging deep into my flesh. He grunts as he jerks me to my feet. I stumble but manage to catch my balance and stand. Wish I could knee him in the head as he removes the rope that held my calves together. Instead, I pretend to be too weak to struggle and meekly obey as he marches me toward a long, low, derelict building that looks like it was once storage units, half dragging me with him.

I don't see any signs of life. No people, no cars, no help. Just the two of us.

But as he reaches past me to open the door, I know that's going to change all too soon. I prepare myself as he pushes me inside.

The interior of the building is dim. The air is musty. Our steps ring hollowly across the cement floor as we walk down a hall, dark caverns gaping on both sides of us.

A collapsed cardboard box lurks at the edge of the shadows. Random bits of trash are strewn about at our feet. Rodent droppings litter the floor, suggesting that we might not be completely alone, but as far as other humans are concerned, it appears empty.

"Hello?" Skunk's voice echoes as he pulls me to a stop.

There's no answer. He mutters angrily as he looks around, searching the shadows around us. Turns his narrowed, bloodshot eyes my way, his gaze drilling into me with hate. I lift my chin, refusing to look away.

The space briefly lights up as the door opens behind us. Though Skunk turns, he keeps a hand on me, holding me in place. I use the opportunity to pull the knife from under my sleeve and adjust my grip, preparing to strike.

The weapon is dull. I'd been planning on sinking it into the vulnerable softness of his gut, but now I debate trying to jab it into one of his kidneys. If I wait, I may lose my chance to draw blood. If I make my move too soon, I may miss an opportunity to inflict more damage.

"I brought the girl," Skunk says. "Did you bring the money?"

His hold on me tightens, though with nerves or excitement I couldn't say.

“Take it out, show it to me,” he orders.

I can only assume that whoever is here to collect me complies.

“Now toss it over.”

This is my chance, and I don’t intend to miss it. Drawing a deep breath, I tense my muscles, getting ready to spring into action. Listen closely for the sound of the package hitting the floor.

When it does, Skunk releases me. I spin, my focus aimed on where I heard the money fall, the knife clenched in my fist. But just as I’m about to throw myself toward the ground, where Skunk is bending over, my gaze flits toward the door, already trying to plan my next move.

In an instant, all the fight goes out of me. It feels like I’ve been tossed into an icy sea, my skin frozen, my body numb.

Because it’s not one of Bianchi’s men I see. It’s my man. And as my eyes latch onto Jake’s, I can only hope they haven’t somehow become one and the same.

CHAPTER 25

My heart flips inside my frozen chest as Jake's eyes meet mine. I try to read what I see there, but I don't have time. Skunk has noticed the knife in my hand. He knows what I intended to do. And he's *not* happy about it.

He straightens up, eyes gone black with anger. His lips curl back from his teeth, hands reaching for me as he snarls, "You b—"

But I'm not looking at him. Barely register the incoming attack. Because I only have eyes for Jake.

I'm frozen as he pulls a pistol from the back of his pants. A gun that I bought him. That he's now raised, aimed in my direction as his mouth forms words I can't hear.

I watch as his finger curls. Jump back as he pulls the trigger. Fall to the ground as the blast of the gun fills the narrow building, echoing off the rafters while my heart spasms erratically inside my chest.

The blood on my shirt is searing hot against my skin. I can't stop staring at the wound, the dark crimson it leaks spreading in a growing pool across the floor, not quite believing my eyes. But it's true.

Jake just inflicted what is sure to be a lethal injury.

He rushes over, falling to his knees beside me. Reaches a hand toward my face tentatively, like I'm a ghost and might vanish at his touch. His thumb brushes feather soft against my cheek, his eyes full of sorrow.

"Are you okay?"

I don't answer. I can't. I only nod.

Jakes turns toward Skunk, runs his fingers through his dark hair, tugging at it as he looks at the dying man with regret. "I told him to stop." A shudder rolls through him as he whispers, "He didn't listen. I couldn't take the chance that he might hurt you."

Twisting back toward me, he clears his throat and says, "We've got to get out of here."

I observe numbly as he plucks the knife from my fist, folding the blade that I struggled so hard to open back into the handle before slipping it into his pocket. He grabs the backpack with the money in it, slings a strap over his shoulder, then scoops me up off the floor.

He takes a big step to the side, avoiding Skunk's outstretched hand as the man makes a feeble attempt to grab him. His moans have grown weaker. There's now more blood outside of his body than in. By the time we reach the door, the man will be dead.

It could have been me. Almost was. Most likely would have been, if not for Jake. All my doubts and worries are temporarily silenced, buried under relief.

I lean my head against Jake's shoulder and close my eyes while he carries me away. Try my best to stay conscious, not wanting to miss a second of the feeling of his arms around me, the heat of the sun on my face as we step outside, the tenderness he uses as he places me ever so gently in the passenger seat of his truck and straps me in.

I'm grateful and relieved—and overwhelmed with questions.

"I'm so sorry." His voice hitches over the words. "I'll cut you loose as soon as we put some distance between us and this place."

I nod my understanding. I want to ask how he found me, but I already know. I just can't comprehend what it means yet.

The seat beneath me is soft, the air is cool, the hum of the tires rolling across the asphalt soothing, like a lullaby. I want nothing more than to sleep right now. Instead, I study the man beside me.

His suit is rumpled. Dark circles ring his eyes. He clearly hasn't shaved in days. His gaze stays in constant motion, darting between the road in front of us to the mirrors and back. Finally, the vehicle slows, bumping onto the shoulder.

"I think we're good. I haven't seen another car in ten minutes," he says, though he's still staring behind us. He swallows hard, then turns to face me. His expression buckles. "This is all my fault, Cassie. I never should have left."

Jake reaches out, gingerly running his palm across my cheek, his fingertips pushing my hair behind my ear. He hisses, making a face.

"You need a doctor."

"No." The word rasps out from my parched throat.

"Cassie—"

I shake my head and croak, "Water."

He fumbles for a mostly full bottle in the cupholder. Uncaps it and holds it to my lips. I try to drink too fast, making myself choke and sputter. Setting the bottle down, he uses his thumb to wipe my chin dry.

A sudden wave of self-consciousness strikes me as I realize what I must look like. Filthy, bruised, covered in blood and probably my own vomit as well. Despite that, he leans forward, pressing a soft kiss against my forehead. Then he opens the glove box.

Pulling out a multitool, he extracts a knife much larger and sharper than the one I'd been trying to use to free myself and makes short work of the rope that binds me. He passes me the water, watching closely as I grasp it in both hands, forcing myself to take tiny sips.

"We have to get moving again. Are you sure you don't need a doctor?"

I nod. And though he gives me a worried look as he pulls back onto the road, he doesn't argue, which is a blessing. Because odds are, I *could* use some medical attention, but judging from the way he's acting, we can't risk it.

This is more than him just being nervous because he killed a man.

He's spooked, his eyes already back to scanning our surroundings like he's being hunted. I suspect that might be true. And, if it is, that whoever's after him is after me as well.

CHAPTER 26

It's too still. Too quiet. Something's wrong. I jerk awake, hands balling into fists as I struggle upright in the seat.

"It's okay." Jake stretches his arm around me, drawing me to him. "I'm here. I've got you. You're safe."

But am I?

Though we're still in his truck, we're no longer moving. And as I stare over his shoulder out the window, it's not the view I expected to see. If he can feel the way my heart just kicked into overdrive, he doesn't let on.

"Where are we?" I ask, pulling away.

The words come out much easier than they had before. My voice sounds more like my own. Though I'm nowhere near recovered, my body feels a bit stronger, my senses sharper, my brain less addled.

"Why aren't we home?"

"We can't go home," he says sadly.

"What do you mean? We have to. What about—"

"I have people looking after the animals for us."

"Who?"

"The vet has the raccoon."

"Ricky," I murmur. Only, I guess since he's a she, Ricki, maybe.

"What?" Jake asks, brow furrowed.

"Her name," I explain. "One of the men who—" I shake my head, not wanting to waste words with needless details. "The raccoon's name is Ricki. But what about everyone else? The rest of the animals?"

"Hal's going to be staying at the sanctuary to take care of them while we're gone."

"Hal? Your security guard from Myers and Kleinman?"

"Yes."

"Does he know what he's doing?"

Jake grimaces. "No. But he has the vet's number. Craig's going to do his best to talk Hal through any problems he has."

I give him a hard look. "That's not good enough. They deserve better than that. Take me home."

"I can't, Cassie."

"Why not?"

"Because it's not safe."

"So?"

He covers his face with his hands and groans. "I just spent the last three days worried that I'd never see you again. Can you please try to work with me on this?"

"Three days?"

I sit back in the seat, swallowing vainly at the lump in my throat.

"Three days," he whispers.

His eyes glisten. His hand wraps around mine, his grip hot and damp and desperate.

"I know this is all my fault and you have no idea

how incredibly sorry I am. For everything. I screwed up. Once this is over, we'll handle things however you want, but until then, let me keep you safe. Please, Cassie. At the very least you need time to recover, regain your strength."

He gives a relieved sigh as I nod.

"The girls. Amelia? Danielle?"

"They're fine. They made it back two days ago."

A wave of nausea sweeps through me, one that has nothing to do with my head injury. If the girls made it home that long ago, why hadn't anyone come out to that cabin to rescue me?

Jake clears his throat, looking away. "You have no idea how much I wanted to tear those woods apart to come get you."

"But you didn't."

"It was too late. That guy back there had already spread the word that he had you and was looking to sell you to the highest bidder. So, I lied to Sheriff Kingston and told him you'd made it back, too. Told him that the Feds had arrested the kidnappers. And I had Marla tell Agent Gellar that the sheriff had them in custody. She convinced Gellar to give you a few days before they questioned you."

The heat leaches from my body, leaving me feeling cold and bloodless.

"You what?"

"I had to, Cassie. I'm so sorry."

There he goes, apologizing again. But for what, exactly? I'm afraid to find out, but I have to know. Trust has never come easy for me. It's a lesson I learned early in life after giving it to too many of the wrong people.

I take deep breaths as I look out the window again. We're in a parking lot, though it's not one that I recognize. I have no idea where we are.

My gaze locks on the only other vehicle present, a white sedan. I don't see the shadow of anyone inside of it, but the driver must be nearby. My hand curls around the door handle.

"Why would you do that?" I ask quietly. "Why would you make sure I stayed out there?"

"To keep you safe."

"How was leaving me out in the middle of the woods with that junkie keeping me safe?"

"Because he was auctioning you off. Once the girls told everyone what happened, how they came to be taken, how random it was, all because of the paranoia of a druggie, I realized that the only way he'd know that you had a price on your head was if you had told him. Which meant that you were still alive."

"And you figured the best way for me to stay that way was to tell everyone who might look for me that I was already safe and sound?"

"Yes."

I glance at the other car again, hoping to see that the driver has returned. They haven't.

"How does that make any sense at all?"

Jake taps the backpack containing the money he used to buy me from Skunk. "I made sure that I was the highest bidder. Two-hundred and fifty thousand dollars."

My mouth drops. I open the bag and look inside. Sure enough, it's filled with wrapped bundles of hundreds. It's more than I've ever seen in one place before. And a tiny part of me can't help but wonder—did he shoot Skunk because the man was coming after me? Or to get the cash back?

"Come on," Jake says. "We need to keep moving. We have to go."

"What do you mean? Go where?" My voice rises several octaves as Jake opens his door and climbs out of the truck. "Why are you getting out?"

This time, as my hand tightens on the handle, it's to keep me inside the vehicle instead of preparing to escape it.

Jake gestures toward the white sedan. "We've got to make sure they can't find us."

I watch as he rounds the truck and opens my door. Holds out his hand to help me down.

My headache has returned with a vengeance, my skull throbbing so hard I can barely keep my eyes open. I'm so tired, so overwhelmed, in so much pain that I can barely think. But I need to make a decision, and fast.

Do I trust him? Just last week there wouldn't have been a doubt in my mind, but now? He didn't just storm off and leave me at the sanctuary, he made the decision to leave me out in the woods in that shack, too. There was no way for him to know for sure that I'd stay safe—or even alive.

But this is Jake.

I look deep into his eyes for a long moment, the beat of my heart matching the seconds as they pass. Then I give a single nod.

He lifts me down from the cab and folds me in a hug. Holds me tight, until I start to believe that everything will be okay.

With a final squeeze, he pulls away. Grabs the backpack of money from his truck. Pulls his phone from his pocket, then hesitates just before he puts it in the glove box. Indecision flashes across his face, followed by sorrow and something else I can't define.

"Here." He holds it out to me. "You better call Marla real quick. Let her know you're okay."

Taking the device, I lean against the side of the truck and place the call. It gets answered after only half a ring.

"Jake?"

Director Marla Jacobson's voice holds a note of panic that I've heard only a few times before—and always because of the jeopardy I've been put in. I try not to think about all the years that might have been shed off the poor woman's life because she cares about me.

"No, it's me."

"Cassidy! Oh thank goodness. Are you okay?"

"Yes."

"Are you safe?"

I meet Jake's gaze as he watches me with concern. Did he know that I needed this? Confirmation that what he said was true, that Marla knew what was going on and was helping him?

The glimpse of hurt I catch on his face as he turns away makes me suspect so. That he knows I have doubts about trusting him. But do I really? I'm suffering my own hurt, but if I suspect, even for a second, that his intentions are anything other than what he wants me to believe, all I have to do is speak the words right now to Marla.

Drawing a deep breath, I say, "Yes. I will be. I just wanted to let you know… I think we're going off the grid for a while."

She exhales heavily. "That's not ideal, but I understand the decision. You'll let me know if you need anything?"

"I will."

Ending the call, I hand the phone back to Jake. Watch as he puts it in the glove box, closes and locks the doors to his truck. Then, wrapping an arm around my shoulders, he leads me toward the white sedan.

"So what's the plan?" I ask. "We can't just run from Bianchi's men until he loses interest."

Jake stiffens beside me. I cast a wary glance at him from the corners of my eyes. A gush of ice water floods through me. He looks completely stricken.

"What aren't you telling me?" I ask, heart kicking at the walls of my chest as I take a big step away, pulling out from under his arm. I come to a stop, waiting for an answer. "Jake?"

He closes his eyes. Squeezes the bridge of his nose and releases a giant sigh before saying softly, "Bianchi's dead. He was stabbed to death Monday morning at the prison."

I rock back on my heels, trying to keep my balance as a curtain of dizziness drops over me. If that's true, then why are we on the run? Why would Jake need to pay a quarter of a million dollars to be the highest bidder to get me back? Had he purposely waited to tell me this until after I had spoken to Marla?

"Then shouldn't this be over?"

He shakes his head sadly. "I'm sorry, Cassie."

Yet another apology, but still no explanation.

"For what?" I ask sharply. "What's going on? I want the truth this time, the full one."

My stomach churns as his gaze meets mine, because whatever it is that he's so sorry about? His agonized expression tells me it's going to be a doozy.

"I'm sorry because it wasn't Bianchi who put out the hit on you." I hear the click of his throat as he swallows hard. The wavering breath he draws. The pure grief in his voice as he says, "It was my mother."

CHAPTER 27

The ground rushes up to meet me as I sit down. Hard. The sound of the ocean fills my ears, a noise that I vaguely recognize as the blood rushing through my head too fast.

Jake's on his knees beside me with a panicked expression. His lips are moving, but I can't hear a word he's saying. I stare at his hands, wrapped around mine. I can't feel him, either.

How long has he known? What part has he played? And why is he only telling me this now? Raising my eyes to his, I blink away the tears clouding my vision, looking for the truth.

"Cassie." His voice is pure anguish as it breaks through my thundering pulse to reach my ears.

"You've been visiting her," I say, my tone cold and distant.

He nods, swallowing hard.

"And you're paying for her legal defense."

"I didn't know she was the one trying to hurt you

when I made the deal with her. And I didn't know what else to do. I was desperate. After what happened with the sniper, I went to see her after her hearing was delayed the next morning. I told her I'd pay for her to be represented by someone other than the public defender if she told me what I needed to know to protect you."

"And you believed her?"

"I didn't know what to believe. Or who. All I knew was that I had to find a way to keep you safe. I was willing to try anything."

"Is that why you went to see your dad?"

His mouth opens and shuts, his surprise that I know about the visit evident.

"Yes," he says. "Partly. When she was first arrested, I—I didn't know how to feel. A part of me couldn't help but be excited to have her back after all these years."

He sits on the ground beside me. Gives me a timid look as he scoots closer to me, squeezing my hand.

"I was so young when she left. The mom I remembered was fun and loving and kind. Not the type of person who would murder her closest friends. But what she did to your parents, it made me realize that maybe I didn't really know her at all. That I needed to speak with someone who did."

"And what your dad told you?"

"Made me realize you might be in danger. So I started visiting her to see what I could find out."

"And?"

"She acted like nothing was wrong. Like we were just catching up under normal circumstances, like she wasn't facing murder charges. She even asked about you when I visited. She seemed to genuinely care, and I thought—"

His head drops. A shudder rolls through him. When

he continues, his voice is choked, thick with regret.

"I fell for it. She had me convinced that my dad must have lied. That she had spoken the way she had about what happened on the recording because she was scared and she thought taking some of the credit for the murders would get her respect from the people she feared."

I bite my tongue to keep from pointing out all the evidence there was to prove otherwise. Jake isn't like me. Not just because of my career and experience with killers, either. He doesn't assume the worst about everyone. Of course he'd want to believe the best about his mom. I shouldn't fault him for that.

"It turns out she was just playing me the whole time."

"How did you figure it out?" I ask.

He looks like he's going to be ill as he admits, "I almost didn't. It was the private investigator I'd hired who found out that someone was trying to sell you to Bianchi. I was already in negotiations to get you back when the gag order was lifted and I found out that he was dead. But I had competition. There was someone else trying to buy you. That's when I knew it had to be her."

"But you can't be sure. It still could have been one of Bianchi's guys, or one of the two men who were arrested for kidnapping you. If no one knew what happened to him—"

Jake shakes his head sadly. "You don't know how badly I wish that were true. But it was her, Cassie. I have proof."

"I'm sorry, Jake."

A small spark catches inside me, quickly turning into a flame. And Jake's devastated expression? That mix of shame and regret and grief that I've worn so many times myself? It causes that flame to flare into an inferno.

"As long as you're okay, that's all that matters. You know that, right?" He cups a hand to my cheek. I cover it with my own. "I'm not sure how she's pulling this off yet. Until I do, we can't risk going back to the sanctuary."

"Then let's go find out."

"I'm not so sure that—"

I point toward the white sedan. "You have a plan, right?"

"A vague one. But you're in no condition to—"

"I'm fine," I insist. "I just need to drink more water. And eat some food."

"There should be some in the car."

That's all I need to hear to propel me into action.

He frowns as I move to get up. "Maybe you should sit for a few more minutes."

"There's no time. If someone's tracing your phone, they'll be tracking that call I made to Marla. We need to get out of here before they find out where we are."

Jake's lips press together in a tight line, but he nods. Wraps an arm under me to help lift me to my feet. He keeps me tucked to his side as we cross the parking lot to the white car.

"Where'd this come from, anyway?" I ask, gesturing toward the vehicle. "Did Marla help you get it?"

"No. Julian did."

I give him a sharp look. "Julian?"

He grimaces. "Yes."

"So you trust him now?"

Jake nods sheepishly.

"How'd that happen?"

"We talked things out."

My stomach clenches as I remember the footage I saw of Julian at the house the day I was taken. "Was this before or after you gave him a black eye?"

"During." He cocks his head, giving me a curious look. "How'd you know about that?"

"I saw him on the security camera knocking on the door." Reaching the car, I watch as Jake feels around the back tire, withdrawing a set of keys. "You want to tell me how violence resolved your trust issues?"

Jake unlocks the door and holds it open for me. I arch my eyebrows, waiting for an answer.

"I said some things I shouldn't have."

"Like?" I prompt.

"I accused him of trying to drive a wedge between us. To steal you from me."

"I'm not a wallet, Jake. I have free will. I make my own choices."

He hangs his head. "I know. And he told me that there's no way you'd ever choose him. But that I was going to lose you myself if I didn't get my head together and be honest with you."

"Hmm. Definitely sounds like an unreasonable response that deserved a violent reaction to me."

"In all fairness, he took the first swing."

He gestures to his jaw, where I notice the dark shadow of a bruise hiding under the thick stubble that's grown in.

"And what'd you say to get him to do that?"

Rubbing the back of his neck, he asks, "Do I have to tell you?"

"No," I decide. "He hit you, you hit him, then what?"

Jake shrugs. "He apologized. Told me that he hadn't realized I had a valid reason for not telling you what was going on. That he figured I was lying to you about being okay about the situation with my mom, and he wanted you to know that wasn't true."

"Why did you lie?" I ask quietly, finally taking a seat in the car.

He squats down in front of me, sets the backpack full of money on the floorboard, and grabs a bottle of water from the back seat, breaking the seal. As he hands it to me, he says, "Because I couldn't bear to tell you the truth."

"Which is?"

"That being with me might be what's endangering you. That the reason your life is at risk is because of me."

He swallows hard, checking the road with a wary expression that suggests he expects to see danger approaching at any moment. Standing, he gives me a grim look before shutting my door gently and hurrying around to the driver's side, sliding behind the wheel.

I wait until the car is in motion before saying, "That's what I don't get, Jake. How are you sure it was your mom that put the hit out on me? What's this proof that you have?"

"The private investigator I hired was able to track down the sniper's bank accounts and get me his financials. I tracked the money. Deposits made to both him and the inmate who killed Bianchi came from the same bank account. One held by Cadence Glover. My mom's middle and maiden names. And there's only one branch. It's in the Keys."

Pulling my seat belt loose, I turn to face him, studying him as he drives. I'm impressed. "Was this information obtained through legal means?"

"Absolutely not."

"Does anyone else know?"

"Only Julian."

"So what's the plan?"

He lifts his gaze from the road long enough to glance at me. For the first time since he stepped inside that abandoned building earlier, he smiles. “We’re going on vacation.”

CHAPTER 28

I'm using my finger to get the last of the crumbs from the bottom of an empty potato chip bag when the Tamiami spits us out in Homestead. Looking over, I catch Jake watching me.

"You still hungry?"

So far, I've had two candy bars, a container of jerky, pretzels, and a party-size bag of BBQ chips. I've eaten every bite of food in the car. Still famished, I nod.

"What are you in the mood for?"

I look down at myself. There's no way I can go inside any place wearing these filthy clothes, especially not a restaurant.

"We'll get takeout," he adds.

"Burritos, then. And enchiladas. And maybe a couple of tacos."

He grins and points at the phone Julian had left in the glove box along with a half-dozen SIM cards. "Why don't you find a spot and place the order. We'll pick it up first."

"First?"

"We're going to need some supplies. Toiletries, clothes… I wasn't able to pack anything before I left. I was too afraid someone might be watching the house. And it'll be less noticeable shopping around here than where we're going."

It's just one more thing that Jake's already thought of. And he's thought of a lot.

From the untraceable car and phone to ditching his truck in a remote parking lot in the opposite direction of our destination. Having Hal, the head of security from his law firm and an ex-Army Ranger, a man he's known—and trusted—for the last decade, keep watch over the sanctuary. Getting Julian to have a fake ID produced for me in the same name as his mom's bank account.

Even the research he's done and the plan he's come up with. For the first time since I've been back in Florida, I don't feel like a bad influence on him. It seems that I'm not the only one who can cause trouble. And there's something insanely sexy about that.

Maybe that speaks to how damaged I am. Or maybe it's more about recognizing the risks he's taking for me. Because even though his career, his freedom, even his life are in jeopardy if we get caught, he hasn't hesitated for even an instant.

And as he follows my directions and pulls into a parking space, I vow to do whatever it takes to keep him safe and make sure we get that chance at happiness together that he's worked so hard for.

I watch him cross the lot, waiting until he's disappeared inside the restaurant before pulling out the ID Julian had made—the one with my picture beside the name Cadence Glover. It's an amazing fake. Holding it to the light, I check the holograms, the optically variable ghost and data, even the gold look-through.

Every safeguard the state has in place to make it nearly impossible to accurately manufacture a legitimate-looking counterfeit has been achieved. It makes me wonder exactly what kind of resources the lawyers at Myers and Kleinman have access to.

And, flipping down the vanity mirror, sighing at what I see, if they can work the same kind of miracles on people. Because the image of me on this ID no longer matches my reflection.

My eyes look too large, my cheeks too gaunt. My coloring is off. Even the shape of my face appears wrong. I gingerly probe the raised bruise above my ear. It feels slightly squishy, like it's filled with fluid, probably blood. Strangely, even though it's incredibly painful to touch, I can't stop pushing on it.

I'm so preoccupied that I don't even notice Jake's approach. My heart jumps into my throat, pushing out a gasp as the car door opens. My cheeks grow hot as Jake looks between me and the mirror. He flips it up, then hands me the bag of food. Leans forward until his mouth is almost touching mine.

"You're gorgeous. All you need is some sleep and a shower."

"And a toothbrush," I say, trying to hold my breath as I speak.

"I'll get right on that." He gives me a kiss anyway, grinning. Gestures over his shoulder toward the Walmart across the lot. "What else do you need?"

"Don't you want to eat while it's hot?"

"I'd rather get this over with and us back on the road first."

A pang of guilt flares up inside me. I'm not the only

one who needs rest. Chances are I've had much more sleep than he has over the last few days, even if some of it counts as unconsciousness.

"I need everything, I guess," I say.

"Clothes, soap, shampoo, toothbrush, toothpaste, a comb…" he trails off.

"Makeup."

"You don't need makeup."

"The bank teller might disagree. Just some concealer."

"The palest shade they have?" he teases.

"Probably," I admit. Then, rasping my nails against his stubble I say, "Razors."

"You don't like the beard?"

"I love it. But it feels like something that might flay my skin off."

"Razors," he confirms with a nod. "Anything else?"

"Nope. Just hurry back."

"You can count on it."

He gives me another kiss, then sets off across the lot. As I watch him go, I'm overwhelmed with a rush of love. But the thought of losing it makes a knot of trepidation form inside my stomach.

What if we're doing the wrong thing?

I have no experience performing undercover work and Jake's a lawyer. Trying to handle this ourselves could be a very big mistake. One that could get us both seriously hurt—or worse.

But do I really trust anyone else to do it? No. Taking care of this issue once and for all doesn't mean as much to anyone else. I need to be the one to make sure that there are no loose ends left dangling to snag us later. And I will.

Opening the glove box to put the ID back, I notice

the tiny plastic bag that held the extra SIM cards is empty. They must have fallen out. Grumbling, I set the bag of food on the driver's seat and lean forward, peering inside as I fish around, but I can only find three.

I empty everything from within, piling it on my lap, but one of the chips is still missing. It must have slipped between some of the papers. One by one I sort through them. There's the bill of sale for the car, purchased in the name of John Smith. A paper with the reservation number and address of the room Julian booked us. And a folder filled with printouts, where I finally find the pesky little chip I was looking for.

But any relief I feel is short-lived. Because there on the top page is a name that makes the little stone-size knot inside my stomach turn into a cannon ball. Don Farris. The sniper who tried to take my life.

The skin on the back of my neck tightens as I realize what I'm looking at. This must be the information Jake's private investigator uncovered that enabled him to find the man's bank accounts. It's the same type of data that I asked Marla to try to get for me. Only, somehow, Jake's PI had managed to get his hands on it before the FBI.

And the man has been impressively thorough. Inside, I find everything from how my would-be assassin found the jobs he took to his marital status and home address—which is on the exact same Key that Jake and I will be staying on.

Each breath feels like a hostage negotiation with my lungs. My jaw clenches, teeth grinding painfully together as I read through the file, doing my best to commit it to memory. What I discover is chilling. Don Farris was a professional hitman. By all accounts, I should be dead right now, like the dozens of others he'd been suspected of killing for his clients over the years.

I turn to the last page, hoping to find a clue as to why I'm not. It can't just be sheer luck. But as I search for the answer, I realize I'm not going to find it. There was a fluke when this sheet printed.

Instead of revealing the finer details of the man's experience, as the previous sentence implied I should find, the words here are illegible, the text bunched tight on the left, widening on the right. It looks like blood spilling from a body, like it had from Skunk's wound. Thoroughly creeped out, I shiver.

Quickly, I shove everything back inside the glove box other than the folder and the last SIM card, which I push down to the bottom of my pocket. I turn to stare at the store where Jake went, its lights shining brightly in the distance.

I don't believe in coincidences, but I do believe in fate. I think that this is a sign. And it's telling me that what Jake and I intend to do isn't going to be nearly as easy as he thinks.

CHAPTER 29

I stare at the entrance to the store across the parking lot, debating whether I should go inside or not. Though the dread in my stomach has been coated with a thick layer of Mexican food, that doesn't stop it from rising up, clawing at the back of my throat.

How long has Jake been? Long enough to worry? Or am I letting my nerves get the best of me?

There's no denying that I'm twitchy. I can't stop chewing on my lip and trying to finger comb the braid out of my hair, which has turned it into one massive dreadlock. By the time Jake finally appears, I feel like a wreck.

My gaze darts between him, as he pushes an overflowing cart toward the car, and the glove box, where the dossier of Don Farris is stowed once again. As soon as he gets close, I hop out of the vehicle and hurry over to him.

"Everything okay?" he asks as I fall into step beside him.

"Yeah. Just thought you might want some help."

"I've got it. But here." He pauses for a moment, rummages through the jumble of bags and pulls out a large bottle of water. Unscrewing the cap, he hands it to me. "I'll load everything. You rest."

I want to argue that I'm fine, but I have to use both hands to hold the plastic liter he just gave me. Even though the meeting at the warehouse earlier today seems ages ago, the truth is, my body still feels like it's back in that shack in the woods, exhausted, thrumming with fear, dehydrated, and weak.

Despite that, I stay, leaning against the back door of the car as he opens the trunk and begins transferring packages inside.

Picking at the label on the water bottle with a ragged nail, I think about the file in the car. The dossier on Don Farris contains the type of information Director Jacobson was working on getting for me. How had Jake's PI managed to find the data so quickly?

Perhaps an even more important question is, what kind of connections does Jake have that allowed him to take the discovery a step further and access the hitman's financial records?

As easy as it would be to ask, I can't bring myself to say the words. I don't want Jake to think I don't trust him. And I don't want him to know that I've read—and memorized—every word of what his PI discovered.

"So, what's the plan, exactly?" I ask, needing to do something to vent some of my frazzled nerves to make space as more worries continue to fizz up inside of me.

"What do you mean?"

"I mean when we get to Key Largo. I'm going to use that ID to pose as your mom, right? To empty out her bank account?"

Jake deposits a handful of bags into the trunk and says, "I'm not sure. I mean, it's one option, yeah, but I don't know if it's the best one. What do you think?"

"I think it's a start."

He pauses, turning to give me his full attention. "If we take her money, she won't be able to pay anyone to do her dirty work. What else do you think we should do?"

I shake my head in response, not sharing the plan that I've started to form, because if the need arises to put it into action, there's not going to be a *we* involved. It's going to a me job.

Jake studies my expression. "What are you thinking, Cassie? Something's bothering you."

"I guess I'm just concerned. What if it isn't enough? Your mom could have money stashed in bank accounts across the country. Or even in other countries, for all we know."

A muscle in his jaw tics. He swallows hard as he sets his hands on my shoulders. "I don't want you to worry. You've been through enough already. I'm not going to let anything happen to you."

Stepping forward, he closes the distance between us, his arms sliding across my back as he holds me close. He whispers against the top of my head, "I promise. One way or another, I'll make sure she can't try to hurt you again."

Something about the way he says it makes my skin tighten. I pull back until I can see his face. "How?"

"It doesn't matter."

"It does to me."

He tries to pull me back into his embrace, but I refuse to move, staring at him for an answer. Finally, he heaves a heavy sigh. "Look, there are ways to make her go away."

"Such as?"

"Like what she did to Bianchi."

That was not at all what I expected him to say. Nor was it what I was trying to get at.

"You don't mean that."

"I think that maybe I do."

"That's not who you are."

"Well, then I guess it's who she drove me to be. Let's forget for a moment that she murdered your parents and abandoned me with an abusive alcoholic. I made it clear to her, Cassie. Repeatedly. You're the most important thing I have in my life, and she still tried to take you away."

I think back to Monday morning, as Janine sat glaring at me in court. Jake being overly affectionate with me was his way of trying to send a message to her, it just wasn't the one I thought. And apparently, it wasn't one she was willing to hear.

"She's made her choices. If it comes down to it, I'll make mine."

"But if it got traced back to you—"

Jake smiles sadly as he cups a hand to my face. "I'm already going to prison."

"What?"

This feeling is worse than being tied up in that shack. Worse than waking up handcuffed in a serial killer's basement. It's like all the light is being sucked from my world, the darkness closing in around me, with no chance that things will ever return to the way they were.

"I'm pretty sure I killed that man earlier."

"You were saving me."

"How are we going to prove that? Both the Feds and

the sheriff thought you were safe. I've watched enough crime shows to know that they'll be able to determine that his time of death happened after I said you were back."

This isn't happening. I'm not going to let it. I spent my entire career solving crimes, which puts me in a unique position to also know how to cover one up.

Falling into investigator mode, I say, "The burden of proof will be on them. What is there linking you to that old storage facility? Do you own it? Did anyone see you there? Did you—"

"The bullet, Cassie. It was fired from a gun registered in your name."

"Is that all?"

"Isn't that enough?"

"No. Jake, you can stop worrying—"

"I can't. I know about bullet striations and how they can be traced back to the gun that fired them. Once they figure out who that guy is and what he did, the first person they're going to look at is you, and if you believe for one second that I'm going to let them think you did it—"

I silence him with a kiss, the kind I dreamed about giving him during all my conscious hours in the shack. When our lips part, I say, "All of our handguns are loaded with frangible ammunition. It's safer for when you shoot indoors because it disintegrates upon impact which means no ricochets. It also means that most police departments don't have the technology or the manpower that would be required to even try and recover trace evidence off the fragments."

He stares at me for a long minute with an expression of shock. Slowly, it morphs into a hopeful half-smile. "Really?"

When I nod, his smile becomes complete. This time, he kisses me, lifting me from the ground until I feel like I'm floating. I do my best to shut off my brain and enjoy the moment—because you never know how many more moments you're going to get. And I don't have the heart to tell him that I suspect the body in the warehouse is the least of our problems.

CHAPTER 30

Dusk is falling by the time we reach our destination. Gravel crunches under the tires as Jake turns into the lot, parking in one of the spots at the far edge of the circle of light cast by the registration office. As I stir, he puts his hand on my arm, shaking it gently, catching me before I slip back into sleep.

"Cassie, wake up."

"Huh?"

"I think we're here."

I startle, straightening up in my seat, now fully awake as his words register. I stare at the small building, then to the property beyond. "What? This place?"

He gives me a wry smile. "I don't know if this is Julian's idea of a joke, or if he's a genius."

"Well, it just might be the last place anyone would think to look for us." Squinting through the window, I stare at the rows of campers visible beyond the gate. "Do you think we'll be staying in one of those?"

"I don't know. I'll go find out."

I let loose a massive yawn as the car door closes behind him, feeling guilty that I fell asleep, leaving Jake the task of navigating alone. I feel even worse that I never got the answers I needed from him, despite suspecting that I already knew what they'd be.

But even if my suspicions are true, that doesn't mean that Jake's plan won't work. It's entirely possible that emptying his mother's bank account will be enough to cut off her reach outside the walls of her cell. Even if it's not, that's going to have to be a problem for another day.

All I want right now is to clean up and rest and enjoy some time with the man I love. Maybe I can even trick myself into believing this is just a vacation, like normal couples have. Don't we deserve that much? The light clicks on as the door opens. Jake's back already.

"That was quick. So what's the verdict?" I ask, hoping my dreams of a long, hot shower in a space bigger than a toolbox aren't going to be dashed.

Jake doesn't answer, just grins as he slips behind the wheel.

"What?"

He shakes his head, still smiling as he starts the engine and puts the car in gear.

"Seriously. What?"

"You'll see soon enough."

I look curiously out the window as he punches in the code to the gate. It swings open and we drive through, moving at a slow crawl as we make our way down a narrow one-way lane lined with RVs and travel trailers.

The campground is clean and well-tended. The aroma of grilled meat mixed with the brine of the ocean drifts inside the car. And as I spot a series of vacation bungalows off to the side, I feel a rush of relief.

But Jake doesn't even look toward the small buildings as he drives down the gravel road past them. I glance at him, forcing down a million questions. Tell myself to have patience, though my hands tighten on my knees as we continue forward. Then, as we round a curve, the ocean comes into view.

I'm knocked almost breathless. Though I grew up only a handful of hours away, I've never been to the Keys before. I left Gator Glade before I was old enough for Butch to approve of me taking road trips that long without him.

Though I'd resented it as a teenager, as strange as it might seem, I feel grateful now, because the best way to describe what I'm seeing is stunning. Everything my gaze settles on is memorable. And I'm glad that I'm experiencing it for the first time, making these memories, with Jake.

The long shadows of dusk can't conceal the beauty of the gemstone-colored sea. Palm trees are darkened silhouettes. A group of pelicans fly in an arrow formation across a sky painted cotton candy colors by the sunset. It looks like something from a dream—a good one, for once.

Jake stops the car and kills the engine. Covers my hand, wrapped around his arm, and squeezes. I hadn't even realized I'd grabbed onto him.

"Do you like it?"

"I love it."

"Remind me to thank Julian when we get back."

"It's amazing. I could look at this view forever. If you can't find me tomorrow morning, this is where I'll be."

"You don't have to wait until tomorrow."

"Mmm. Priorities. If I don't take a shower soon, the CDC is going to come quarantine me."

"You might be able to see it from the bathroom. I don't know where the windows are, but we'll find out soon enough."

"Wait, we're staying here?"

I tear my attention from the sea and turn it to the building we're parked beside.

"Yes."

"Isn't that a clubhouse or something?"

"It's their honeymoon suite."

"Are you kidding?"

"Not at all."

"Oh, you owe Julian a *very* big thank you."

I hop out of the car, but as I gain my feet, I discover the surge of energy I felt from excitement doesn't extend to my body. I catch myself on the door as I stumble, my legs threatening to give out.

"Whoa. Hey."

Jake hurries around to my side and scoops me up in his arms.

Eyeing the steps that lead inside, I say, "I can walk. I just need a moment."

"Honeymoon suite, remember?"

A lump lodges in my throat as he carries me toward the front, which I can now see is a solid wall of opaque glass. This place is unbelievable. Gorgeous. Magical. Romantic. And here I am feeling like a pile of matted fur that baked in the sun for days before being scraped off the side of the road and not looking much better.

As if he can read my mind, Jake says, "You need a hot shower and a good night's sleep. We have a long day tomorrow."

"But—"

"Tomorrow," he says, handing me the keys so I can unlock the door. My relief and disappointment collide as he carries me over the threshold and I see the inside, where the view is no less breathtaking.

As soon as he sets me down, I find myself drawn to the glass wall, still entranced by the view. Jake follows, wrapping his arms around me. Leaning back against him, I release a happy sigh. We watch in silence as the sun sinks below the horizon and the night sky darkens. Then I look up at him and smile.

"Go start the water. I'll bring the toiletries in first so you'll have what you need."

I grab his arm as he releases me to keep him from leaving.

"Are you okay?" he asks.

"Yeah. I just wanted to say thank you. For everything. I'm really glad that we're here together."

"Me too."

My eyes stay on him while he returns to the car as I try to fix this memory—this man, this place, this feeling—in my mind forever. Then I force myself to turn away.

I'm going to do my best to enjoy our time here. To not do the me thing and get trapped inside my head amid the dark thoughts. But I can't let my guard down, either, not even for a second.

Because there's danger out there in the darkness, lying in wait. I can feel it. No matter how much I want to pretend, I can't. It's a lesson I've learned too many times the hard way—bad things happen, even in the places you'd least expect them to.

CHAPTER 31

The sound reaches inside my dream. At first, it's just there in the background, a gentle stroke, easily ignored. But it gains the insistence of a poke. Then the momentum of a shove, until I'm fully awake, eyes peeled wide against the dark, covers clenched in my fists as I struggle to control the rapid pounding of my heart.

Slowly I sit up, and yet the noise persists, the tap, tap, tapping of a finger against the glass. Then, with a sigh of relief, I place it. Rain. And I must finally be rehydrated, because the sound of it has my bladder begging for release.

Swinging my legs over the side of the mattress, I peer into the shadows of the unfamiliar room around me, noting the location of the furniture before I stand. The nightstand beside me, a chair in the corner, a dresser by the bathroom door—the place where I'd watched Jake set the phone to charge as I was falling asleep.

I glance over my shoulder, watch the gentle rise and fall of his chest for a moment before slipping from the bed. The tiles are cold beneath my feet as I tiptoe across them. The cell feels warm in my hand as I cover the screen before unplugging it from its charger.

Continuing my journey to the bathroom, I close the door silently behind me. Wince as I press the button to lock it and it engages with a click. I freeze, listening for any sign that I've woken Jake. When there's none, I feel around in the pitch-black until I find my damp towel from earlier.

Rolling it into a cylinder, I tuck it into the crack beneath the door, then turn the device on, using the light to locate my filthy pants, still on the floor in the corner. Checking the pocket, I find the SIM card I'd placed there earlier. Then, sitting to relieve myself, I begin my search.

It's an odd experience, learning about the person who's tried to kill you. I've done it before, but this time feels different. Because the deeper I dig, the more my assailant seems less like a monster and more… human.

Despite being a contract killer, he had a wife. Children. A dog. And based on the photos on his spouse's Facebook page, a large extended family and a lot of friends. I study their faces in the glow from the screen, wondering who it is—which one of these connections of his might die at my hands?

Is it the man with the receding hairline? The woman with the tiny gap between her front teeth? Or maybe I'm wrong and the person I'm looking for isn't in any of these pictures. The only thing I know for sure is that they exist.

Because the information Jake's private investigator gathered on him, the dossier I found in the glove box of the white sedan, contains a vital piece of information and that's how Don Farris found the jobs he took.

I scroll through his wife's feed, ignoring everything

else. The cold that starts to take me in its grasp. My fatigue and the overwhelming urge to return to bed. Even my guilt at keeping what I've discovered from Jake.

He's been so hopeful that his plan will work, that we can take away his mother's means to hire another hitman and end this once and for all. And I'd love for that to be true. But there's one thing that makes me fear that it won't be that simple.

According to the intel in the file, the sniper refused to communicate any way other than in person. No paper trail, no risk of a phone conversation being recorded, no electronic footprints that could lead back to him.

Though I wouldn't put it past Janine Walker to have the gall to invite an assassin to visit her in prison to discuss murder for hire, she couldn't have. She's still under the restrictions of a new inmate, limited to visits only from immediate family and legal counsel.

Which means that Janine Walker didn't hire him. Someone else did it for her. And until I figure out who that person is, this won't truly be over.

Goosebumps rise to the surface of my skin, spreading across my flesh as I shiver. It has nothing to do with being chilled. At least, not in the temperature sense.

As a family man, it makes sense that Don Farris was cautious, but as careful as he was, it turns out that he wasn't careful enough.

My heart pounds against the walls of my chest in outrage. It sounds like a drum, filling my ears with an almost deafening echo. Looking at the bathroom door, I half expect to see Jake standing there.

It's still closed. Still locked. But that doesn't mean I don't have to do this quickly.

Clicking on a photo of Don Farris, a candid shot that

he doesn't seem aware was being taken, I spread my fingers across the screen to enlarge the man beside him. Stopping before the picture gets too grainy, I capture a screenshot. Close out Facebook and run an image search using Google Lens.

Within minutes, I've navigated to the Monroe County Tax Collector's website. Searched variations of Janine's name, including the alias we know she uses. Then I enter the identity of the man from the Facebook photo. A list populates with three different properties in the county owned in his name.

I read the addresses over and over, committing them to memory until when I close my eyes, I can still see them. And the man's face.

There's a hollow ache inside me as I break off a tooth from the comb Jake bought me, using it to remove the SIM card from the phone. I insert the replacement, then use the lid from the toilet tank to crush the used one before dropping the pieces down the sink drain.

Clearing the search history on the phone, I power it off. Once my eyes have adjusted to the dark, I remove the towel from beneath the door, disengage the lock, and open it. Put the cell back on the charger. Then I creep across the room.

As I climb back into bed, scooting across the mattress closer to Jake in hopes of absorbing some of his warmth, I take solace in the fact that he'll never suspect a thing. He trusts me—the same way that I should trust him.

CHAPTER 32

The sun beats down from above. The heat is stifling, sweat prickling along my spine and beading along my hairline. My palm, cupped against Jake's, is damp.

Despite that, I feel chilled as we trek the half mile from where we decided to park to the bank. And though we talked our game plan over for hours this morning, the band tightening around my chest with each step gives me the sense of being unprepared.

As we step inside, it only gets worse. I shiver against the frigid air conditioning, goosebumps racing across my body. The bare skin of my shoulders, revealed by the sundress Jake bought for me, feels like it's shrinking against my bones.

I want to turn around and retreat. Instead, I fix a smile on my face and remind myself to keep my head held high as we get in line.

Fluorescent lights flicker overhead, threatening to trigger a headache. My left eye twitches, reminding me to pull my hair forward, over my bruised temple. Even with the wound covered, I still look rough. Though the concealer Jake bought helped, it was unable to perform the miracle of making me look like a human in full health.

Maybe that's why I can't help feeling like this is a long shot. That there's no way, despite the perfect replica of a Florida state driver's license with my picture next to the name of the account holder, that this is going to work.

Yet as we step up to the counter and a young woman in her twenties with spiky hair asks how she can help us, my voice is clear and confident, as I reply, "Yes, I'd like to close out my account please."

"Certainly."

As she types on her keyboard, my gaze drifts to the other clerk trapped behind the Plexiglass with her. I watch the man unwrap a lollipop from the small bowl between them and shove it into his cheek before he pulls out his phone. A tattoo is just visible on his neck, above the collar of his short-sleeved button-up shirt.

"And do you have your debit card with you, ma'am?" the teller assisting me asks.

"Shoot. I knew I forgot something," I say.

Jake, per our prearranged strategy, says, "Cadence, I reminded you before we left. I'm sorry, ma'am. She'd forget her head if it wasn't attached."

"I know my account number, if that helps," I offer, along with an apologetic smile.

"Do you have your ID on you?"

"I do."

I pull it out of my dress pocket and slide it to her.

"Since you don't have your debit card with you, I'll need you to enter your Social Security number for me."

I tap the number I memorized this morning into the keypad.

"Thank you, Ms. Glover."

Her coworker's head snaps in my direction.

"And how would you like the funds?"

"A cashier's check, please," I say, pretending I didn't notice the way I gained the tattooed man's attention the instant she said the name Glover, his gaze latching onto me with undisguised suspicion.

He gives me a long, hard stare, his eyes narrowing before he walks to the end of the teller station. His focus stays on me as he lifts his cell to his ear. My heart races, galloping like a runaway horse as I realize what's happening. Instinctively, I reach for Jake's hand but stop myself before I make contact.

I peek at him from the corners of my eyes. He appears not to have noticed the man's strange behavior. The man who's still staring, his scrutiny needling its way beneath my skin. It would be better if it stayed that way.

"And who would you like that made out to?" our clerk asks.

Clearing my throat, I say, "Cash, please."

She nods and continues typing. It won't be long now. Just a few more minutes and Jake and I can get out of here. Feeling emboldened, I look right at the man and smile. He doesn't return it. "Also, would it be possible for me to get a closing statement?"

"Of course. I'll print off a copy of all recent activity that's occurred since your account last totaled."

"Thank you. How long will I continue to have access to my statements online?"

"I'm afraid you won't once the account closes."

"Oh." I act like it's a surprise.

"Will that be an issue? I can see if I can print off your last few statements for you, if that will help."

Resisting the urge to ask how long it will take, I say,

"That would be great."

Deep breath in. Deep breath out. I pretend that nothing is wrong because nothing is—yet.

Jake's hand touches against the damp fabric at the small of my back. Glancing at him, I find he's noticed that I've drawn the tattooed man's attention. But he doesn't know why. And I don't want the man looking at Jake too closely.

I squeeze between Jake and the counter, drawing his focus and keeping it on me until his back is angled to the guy. Then I lean against him, tucking myself under his arm like I'm using him as a shield, the way you might when a creepy stranger is making you uncomfortable by looking at you a little too intensely.

"Here you go, ma'am. Is there anything else I can help you with today?"

The teller tucks the cashier's check into an envelope and passes it, along with a stack of printouts, across the counter.

"No, thank you."

"Then I hope you have a great rest of your day."

"Thanks. You too."

Grabbing Jake's hand, I lead him toward the exit, forcing myself to keep my pace slow and measured. Doing my best to keep his face angled away from the tattooed man. I glance over my shoulder to find him off the phone but still watching me. Our eyes meet as he says something to his coworker, then disappears from view.

A moment later, the door to the back opens. He's following us. Or, at least, he's going to try. As soon as we've left the building, I quicken my steps, tugging Jake in the direction opposite the one we parked.

"Where are we going?"

"Detour," I say, pulling him into a shop just as the

man emerges from the bank. He jogs around the side, toward the parking lot. We need to kill some time. It won't take him long to figure out his mistake, and I don't want to be on the street when he does—we'll be too easy to spot.

"How many?" a voice from behind me asks.

I jump. Turn to find a hostess watching us expectantly. Shoot a questioning look at Jake, who shrugs.

"Two."

She leads us to a nearby table, much too close to the glass windows, where we could easily be spotted from outside.

"Actually, do you have anything maybe a little more… private?" I ask.

"We're on our honeymoon," Jake adds.

The annoyed expression on her face eases as she looks between us.

"Sure."

A minute later, we're tucked into a booth at the very back of the restaurant. As soon as she's gone, he asks, "Now, do you want to tell me what this is really all about?"

I don't. So I answer his question with one of my own. "Do you want to wait until we get back to the car to look?"

Instantly, the menu in his hand is forgotten about. "No. How much is it?"

I slide the envelope across the table to him. My stomach clenches at his expression as he looks at the cashier's check inside.

"What?"

A crease forms between his brows. His head shakes slowly from side to side. Slowly, he withdraws the slip of paper and lays it on the table, turning it so I can see. It's for a hundred and forty-nine dollars and seventeen cents.

It could be that Janine's out of money. Or that murder for hire is a lot cheaper than you'd expect. But I suspect the truth is that this is just the tip of the iceberg. And like the Titanic, sometimes it's what you can't see that sinks you.

CHAPTER 33

My stomach twists and turns. Just speaking about food as I place my order makes me feel like I might be sick. I don't have an appetite anymore. It's hard to believe that I'll ever be hungry again. But I know I need to keep my strength up.

I smile at the server before she scurries away to place our order, obviously eager to get away from what she must have sensed was a tense situation. Given what Jake told the hostess about us being on our honeymoon, I can only imagine what they might be whispering about us. Luckily, I don't have to think about it for long.

As soon as she's gone, Jake leans across the table, keeping his voice low as he says, "That whole conversation in the parking lot last night. Now it makes sense. You knew."

"I didn't know."

"Cassie, don't give me that."

"I didn't know," I repeat.

"But you suspected." When I nod, he asks, "How?"

"While you were in the store, I found the file on Don Farris in the glove box."

"When you first went missing, I called Marla," he explains. "We had no idea what had happened to you, but she told me about the information that you had asked her to try and find out about him. That's when I asked my PI to do a deep dive into his background, in case you'd discovered something that led to your disappearance."

I nod. "I wanted to know everything I could about him. Specifically, how he got hired for his hits. If he had a handler who arranged things, or if there was a message board or website that he used, anything that might help me to stay ahead of another attack."

Trying to ignore how pale Jake looks, I focus on the salt and pepper shakers, spinning them in my hands.

"According to the file, the authorities had attempted to bring charges against him on two separate occasions," I say. "Both times, they were offering reduced sentences to some of his known associates in exchange for testifying against him. But they could never make the charges stick because they had no actual proof."

"I saw that," he confirms. "But I still don't understand how that let you know my mom's account would be empty."

"Like I said, I didn't know. But when I read that they had no proof because Farris refused to discuss any jobs other than in person, that even though they knew what he was doing, they couldn't prosecute him for it because it was just one criminal's word against another, it clicked."

Jake closes his eyes, drawing a deep breath as he makes the connection as well. "If he only made deals in person, that means he either went to the jail to speak with my mom, or that she has someone on the outside who did it for her."

"Yes."

"Why didn't you say anything?"

"Because I was hoping I was wrong."

He tents his hands over his nose, eyes squeezed shut.

"Jake, we'll figure something else out."

"I already have."

"What?"

"I wasn't lying when I said I'd take care of her, even if I have to do it with my own hands."

"Don't talk like that."

"It's true."

"It's not. You're just venting."

"I don't think that I am, Cassie. If I have to choose between keeping you safe—"

"You're upset. I get that." Reaching across the table, I cover his hand with mine. "But the man I love wouldn't actually do something like that."

Only, the man sitting across from me right now looks like he just might. I need to put a stop to this, no matter what it takes. I can't let Jake throw his life away just because I became a part of it. Seeing him like this, knowing it's because of me, is almost enough to make me regret coming back home.

"The man you love doesn't deserve you," he mumbles.

"Are you kidding me?" I laugh, but he won't meet my eyes. "How can you even say that? You've always been there for me when I've needed you."

"I wasn't there for you when you decided to go into the woods on your own."

"It was my decision to do that. Obviously, it was a bad one. I knew it was stupid. And to be honest, it was more because I was mad at Sheriff Kingston than you."

"Yeah, well, I'm sure the part I played didn't help any."

"We had an argument, Jake, and as I recall, I wasn't entirely blameless for it."

"Yeah, but you're the one who kept calling and trying to apologize. I chose to ignore you."

"It wasn't like I didn't know where to find you. Do you think Hal really could have kept me out of the building if I decided I wanted in?"

"It's doubtful."

His lips twitch. It's not a smile, but it's a start.

"We're going to figure this out." Tapping the stack of printouts, I say, "We have a paper trail here to follow. All the money going in and out of that account for the last three months. That's going to tell us what we need to know."

"But how long is that going to take?"

I shrug and give him a small smile.

"What's the rush?"

"I know you're anxious to get back to the sanctuary."

I am. Just thinking about the animals makes my heart clench. But returning now would just be putting them in danger. I can't go home, not until this is over. Neither of us can.

Leaning closer to him over the table, I say, "That was before I knew we were on our honeymoon."

His fingers tighten around mine. "You're right. No one knows we're here. We're safe for now."

The lump in my throat tastes like poison as I swallow it down. A toxic mix of shame and deceit. Because after our stunt at the bank today, they do know. They know, and now the element of surprise I'd been expecting to have is gone.

Which means that the situation has become even more dangerous. Whatever confidence I had felt before has vanished. But if I think about it too much, I'll psych myself out. I can't let that happen. I need to stay distracted until the time comes for me to rush headlong into trouble the way I usually do.

"Let's take the rest of today off," I suggest. "Try to relax and unwind and enjoy ourselves."

"How do you propose we do that?" He gives me that lopsided grin of his, the one that's been hiding for far too long.

"Let's go for a walk after lunch. Dip our toes in that gorgeous water I keep seeing."

I do my best to sell the smile I give him. To not reveal that on the inside, I'm reeling. I have to find a way to put my worries aside. Tonight, I need to focus on nothing but Jake and enjoying our time together. Because if Janine and her cohort get their way, we don't have very much of it left.

CHAPTER 34

It's the kind of day you never want to end. After lunch, we took a long walk on the beach, which led to us ducking into a tourist shop for bathing suits, a blanket, towels, and an umbrella for me to hide under when we weren't in the water. We splashed and played. Kissed and held hands.

When Jake noticed that my energy was starting to flag and suggested we head back to the campground for the night, I didn't want to go, insisting I was fine. It was only when I fell asleep on the blanket that I was forced to concede, and even then, it was only because he had already carried me halfway to the car by the time I woke.

Though it makes me nervous that my body is still so in need of rest that I could sleep that deeply, I push back the concern, not wanting to ruin what's been a perfect afternoon. And it really has been perfect.

"Why don't we grab a pizza on the way back?" I suggest.

"No, I'll go back out and pick one up. I want to drop

you off first."

"What am I going to do there by myself? Why don't I come with you?"

"Why don't you take a bath and relax?"

One thought of the two-person jetted tub in the honeymoon suite's bathroom and any resistance I planned to put up was forgotten. And as I lie here now, soaking, my knotted muscles slowly unwinding, it feels exactly like what I needed. Until I wake up in tepid water with no idea how much time has passed.

Water sloshes as I bolt upright, heart racing, my first thought Jake. Grabbing a towel, I rush into the bedroom in a panic. It's only when I hear him moving around on the other side of the door that it's replaced by guilt for napping when we could have been spending time together.

Quickly, I pull on the oversized T-shirt he bought me to sleep in and a pair of underwear and go to join him. I only get several steps down the hall before I draw to a stop.

A blanket is spread on the floor in front of the window wall. Two wine glasses and a couple of plates sit in the center.

"What's all this?" I ask, propelled back into motion.

Jake leans his head around the corner of the kitchen and smiles.

"I thought we'd have a picnic. Take a seat. I'll be there in a sec."

I feel dazed as I settle onto a corner of the blanket. Stare out the window as I wait for him to join me.

Outside, the sun hovers just above the water. Lavender clouds streak a sky the same pink as the inside of the conch shell I found on the shore today. This—all of it—is enough to take my breath away.

"You're just in time," Jake says, gesturing toward the sunset as he carries over a box of pizza and two bottles of wine. He fills my glass before taking a seat across from me. Doesn't mention how long he must have had to wait for me as he holds open the box, waiting for me to take a slice before putting one on his own plate.

As the first bite of cheesy goodness fills my mouth, I can't help moaning. I don't know if the pizza's that good, or if I'm just that hungry, but, in this moment, it's the best thing I've ever tasted.

We eat in silence, eyes locked on the sun as it slowly sinks below the horizon, the clouds backlit with an ethereal glow as the last of the light shimmers off the water. I feel myself gasp as there's one last startling flash, igniting across the sky like a hungry flame.

In the blink of an eye, it's gone. The show's over. It's only then that I notice the tiny box half concealed in the center of the blanket.

"What's that?" I ask, pointing at it.

"Why don't you open it and find out?"

Jake's face is uncharacteristically blank as I reach out and take the small black velvet container in my hand. My fingers shake as I open it. My heart leaps up into my throat as I see what's inside.

"What is this?" I ask, so quietly it's almost a whisper.

"It's a ring."

"I know that. But what's it for?"

"To wear."

I'd roll my eyes, but I can't seem to tear them away from the piece of jewelry.

"Where'd it come from? Did you buy it?"

"Yes."

"For me?"

"Yes."

I feel dazed as my mind struggles to make sense of what's happening. I inspect his face for the answer, but it's still curiously neutral as he studies me back.

"Is this? I mean. Why?"

Jake shrugs. "I saw it in a shop while I was waiting for the pizza. I figured since we might be staying here for a while, you should have a ring. So people won't have questions about us staying in the honeymoon suite."

The lump in my throat is so large I can barely speak. "So it's not…?"

"It's just a cheap trinket."

Only, it's not. It might not be a diamond, but it's beautiful. A trillium cut stone, a Ceylon sapphire, I think, held in its setting by waves made of tanzanite. Maybe it's not what some women would want, but to me, it's perfect. And to hear him call it a trinket, to learn that it's not what I thought it was—though I expected to be relieved, I'm not sure that I am.

Over the course of my life, I haven't spent much time thinking about getting married. My career always came first. There was never anyone who made the idea of giving up my independence seem worthwhile. Until now. I swallow hard, not sure what to say.

"You don't have to wear it," Jake says.

The box trembles as I hold it out to him. I'm not sure if it's my imagination or not that it still trembles as he takes it from me. My left hand darts out, hovering above it.

"Are you kidding? I love it. Put it on me."

Jake's face lights up like a kid on Christmas morning as he lifts the ring from its velvet bed and slips it onto my finger. It's a perfect fit. And I can't help smiling as I hold my hand up, admiring it.

"Do you really like it?" Jake asks shyly.

Shoving the pizza box to the side, I push up onto my hands and knees. Crawl over the blanket to him and kiss him like the world is ending.

"Cassie, you're still recovering. We don't have to—"

I cut him off with another kiss that makes my intentions clear. His hands glide down my hips, slipping under the bottom of my shirt. Grasping my backside, he lifts me onto his lap. Straddling him, I thread my fingers through his hair while his hands roam my body like he's trying to memorize every inch.

I'm at risk of overheating, and yet I shiver as my shirt comes off. Moan softly as his lips trace over my skin. And wish, with everything in me, that this moment would never end.

CHAPTER 35

I'm woken by a flash. A moment later there's another as a bolt of heat lightning streaks across the moonless sky. Dark clouds have gathered, blocking out the stars.

I stare into the blackened room around me, listening. Hear only the soft sounds of Jake's breathing as he sleeps curled around me, one arm pillowing my head, the other draped across my chest. Another bolt of electricity forks across the sky, revealing the stark contrast between the dark tan of his skin against the pale curves of my breasts. Then I'm shrouded in darkness again.

I wish I could stay here forever. In this place, in this moment, in the arms of the man I love. It almost kills me that I can't. But the threat of death is greater if I do.

Gently, I lift his arm and wiggle out from beneath it. Whisper the word "bathroom," in case I've stirred him to consciousness. Stand there, looking down at where I know he lies just long enough for the room to illuminate again, searing the image of him as he sleeps into my brain, before I creep down the hall.

Shutting the door to the bedroom, I turn on one of the lamps, using the light to dress. Locate the pad of paper and pen I found earlier and use it to scribble a note.

I love you more than I would have ever thought possible. Please don't be mad. I'll be back as soon as I can, and this will all be over. ~ C

I pray that it's true as I grab the car keys off the dresser. The gun from beneath the mattress. Some cash from the backpack stashed on a shelf in the closet. Stare at the phone, finally deciding to leave it in case I'm wrong and I fail and Jake needs to call for a way out of here.

Then I turn the lamp off, feeling my way in the dark until I find the back door. Inch it open. Turn the lock on the knob so it will latch as I pull it closed behind me.

The sounds of the car seem painfully loud against the still of the night. Every crunch of gravel beneath the tires makes me flinch as I crawl down the narrow lane, trying not to disturb any of the campers. Finally, I pull out onto the road. I make it only a mile before I pull over, blinded by the tears that stream hot and thick down my cheeks.

I punch the steering wheel as I cry, loud, angry sobs that wrack through my body. I weep at the pain of leaving like I did, without even a goodbye. At the unfairness of it all. How hurt Jake will be when he wakes to find me gone. And how angry I am that any of this is necessary in the first place. It's this emotion that I use to pull myself together.

Wiping my eyes dry, I continue my journey. The clock on the car dashboard tells me it's just after 3 a.m. It will be hours before anything opens. But I'm going to need every moment of that time. Without the phone's GPS app to navigate with, I'll have to drive around, searching for the places that I need.

Time seems to stand still as I journey across a series of islands connected by a string of narrow bridges, all of which I appear to have to myself, yet before I know it, the indigo sky is paling. I make my stops. Collect my purchases. Have found a place for the car and a spot to hide before the heat of the new day has had a chance to gather.

So much of this relies on chance. If one thing goes wrong, the rest of the pieces of my plan will collapse like dominoes set into motion. That's why I can't let anything go wrong.

I have to take my time. Do things right. Even if my bladder feels like it's going to burst by the time I step out of the bushes and place the barrel of the pistol I hold snugly between the man's ribs.

He yelps. Tries to twist away, but I already have my other hand clenched in a fist around his belt.

"Quiet. If you do as I say, I won't kill you. Do you understand?"

His shaggy hair flops as he nods.

"Good. Now we're going to turn around—slowly—to face the back of the parking lot. Then we're going to go through the hedge to the other side. Got it?"

Another nod.

"All right. Let's go."

We move as one, branches scraping against us as we squeeze through a gap hardly wide enough for an underfed alley cat. But getting to the other side is only a fraction of this battle.

"Get in the car. The driver's side."

I slip into the seat behind him as he gets behind the

wheel.

"Take out your phone. Turn it on, set it on the console, then put your hands on the wheel."

I wait until he's done as I've said, then I take the device and go into the settings to disable the screen lock.

"What do you plan to do?" he asks.

He pales, recognition dawning across his face as I make eye contact with him in the rearview mirror. I smile.

"Don't worry about that."

Opening his contacts, I scroll, but don't see the name I'm looking for.

"What do you have Garrett's number saved under in here?"

"Uh-uh. There's no way I'm telling you that. He'll kill me if I do."

"Did he tell you who I am?"

"Yeah."

"Then you should know that you won't have to worry about him by the time I'm done."

His mouth drops open, but no words come out.

"It doesn't matter," I say. "You probably weren't smart enough to delete the call after you placed it."

Sure enough, there's a call in the log that corresponds with the time Jake and I were in the bank yesterday saved under the name Mr. G, though whether the G stands for Garrett or Glover I couldn't say.

All I know for sure is that the man who'd been caught in the Facebook photo with the hitman, the one a Google Lens search identified as Garrett Glover, looks too much like Jake for comfort. Considering that he's using Janine's maiden name, the one she chose for the account at the bank, it makes sense that they're related. But how closely are they connected?

The pictures I found online were all too old or blurry for me to determine what age he might be. I tried searching vital records, but I didn't even know what town to search, so it's not surprising that I was unable to find anything.

As much as I've longed to ask Mallory for help, to see what she can uncover about the man, to at least find out whether Garrett Glover is his real name or an alias, I can't. I don't want to put my friend in danger, and this? It's a big steaming pile of it.

So I'm forced to go in blind. For all I know, Janine had another son after she left Gator Glade. This man, Garrett, could be Jake's younger brother.

Which means that no matter how badly I want to end this with violence, I need to do my best not to let it escalate to that. Because if Jake does have a sibling he's never met before, I can't be the one to take that opportunity away from him.

The tattooed teller in the seat before me lifts a hand.

"Don't," I say.

"I have an itch."

"Too bad. How well do you know Janine?"

"Who?"

"Cadence Glover?"

"That's a real person?"

I stifle a groan. This guy doesn't strike me as smart enough to be lying.

"How many accounts does Garrett have at your bank?"

He shakes his head, refusing to answer.

"We can do this the easy way, or the hard way."

Still, he's silent.

"You leave me no choice."

I press the green icon next to the phone number to

dial. Wait several rings, my nerves ratcheting with each one of them, until the call is answered.

"Eddie, my man, what's up?"

"This isn't Eddie," I say, meeting the bank teller's frantic gaze in the mirror and smirking. "He thought I should make this call myself."

There's a long drawn out pause that I take for shock, but when the man speaks, his voice sounds amused, like he's on the verge of laughing. "Cassidy Knox."

"Garrett Glover."

"You are a crafty one, aren't you?"

"I'm highly motivated. And I'm on my way to a warehouse listed in your name on the tax roll. You know the one I'm talking about?"

"I do."

"Then how about you meet me there in ten minutes?"

"It would be my pleasure."

"Come alone, no weapons, and we'll keep the chat friendly."

Hanging up, I use the phone to tap the tattooed man on his shoulder. "I guess now you're better off with me surviving than him. Here, take this and get out of the car."

"What are you going to do to me?"

"Nothing."

He turns to face me with a startled expression. I hand him his phone.

"I'm not the bad guy here. You should remember that."

His Adam's apple bobs as he swallows hard, giving a single nod before he jumps out of the car like he's afraid I might change my mind. The truth is, I don't want to hurt anyone. But that doesn't mean I won't.

CHAPTER 36

I should have known that my luck wouldn't hold. Should have expected something like this to happen. But I'd been so desperate for everything to be quick and easy. To put this nightmare behind me so Jake and I could get on with our lives—happily and together.

Now, it feels like a clawed fist just seized my heart in a stranglehold and clenched, the tips of the daggered nails puncturing the vital organ. Because even though I'd been so careful, tried so hard, it feels like my plan is crumbling to pieces.

But it's too late to turn back now.

While I was driving around before dawn, learning my way around, I timed the drive between the house listed in Garrett's name on the tax roll and the warehouse. It should have taken him a full fifteen minutes to get here.

Though it only took me six minutes to make the drive from the parking lot behind the bank, it was clear the instant that my destination came into sight that something unexpected had happened. Because the same car that had been parked outside Garrett's house, a very recognizable classic Mercedes convertible, silver with a black soft top, is already here now.

Which means I have no chance to prepare. No opportunity to lay a trap. No time to take measures to ensure that I have the upper hand.

Instead, I just have a sick feeling of dread filling my insides to capacity and the sinking sensation that this is only the first thing that will go wrong. I wish I could turn around, drive back to the campground and pretend this never happened, but I can't do that. I have to at least try to seize back control of my life, my safety, my future.

I glance around quickly, surveying my surroundings as I come to a stop in front of the building. There's not much more than I was able to see in the dark this morning. Several other similar structures are arranged around a property that otherwise appears abandoned.

Weeds break through cracks in the asphalt and crowd around the sides of the warehouses, which are simple and nondescript, exact replicas of each other. There are no windows. An oversized single door has been cut into one of the two-story corrugated metal walls of each building. There are no trash cans, no benches, not even lights affixed to the exteriors by the entries.

I decide to leave the keys inside the ignition in case I need to make a quick getaway, but that leaves the problem of where to put my gun. I'm the one who said no weapons. I can't exactly go waltzing in there with a firearm, not if I want any credibility that I'm here to make nice. And I don't want to leave it in the car if it's going to be unlocked.

My legs tremble as I exit the vehicle, knowing that I'm out of time. I fill my pockets with the one surprise I have going for me and hurry toward the door. There are only two options for where to stash the pistol. Beneath the chunk of concrete beside the door, probably used to prop it open when deliveries are being made, or the weeds. I choose the weeds.

Turning to check behind me, making sure I'm not being observed, I tuck the gun beneath the leaves of a thick dandelion. Then, taking a deep breath, I brace myself, wrap my hand around the knob, and open the door.

The interior is dim. Though strings of bare bulbs zigzag across the ceiling, only the center row has been turned on, leaving the sides of the building in shadows.

It's hot, despite several ventilation fans spinning slowly on the ceiling. Towering stacks of boxes and crates crowd the room, creating ample places to hide. The man I'm here to meet must be using one of them, because he's nowhere in sight.

I force myself to take a step inside, then another. The door closes behind me with a bang, casting the room in further darkness. The familiar fingers of a panic attack trace icy fingers along my neck. I draw deep breaths, trying to keep them from wrapping around me with a choking squeeze.

"That's far enough."

The voice startles me, even though I was prepared for it. I turn toward the corner where it came from, peer into the darkness between two shipping crates. Garrett Glover emerges from between them. Even through the gloom I can see the smirk on his face. And the pistol in his hand.

"So you're the woman I've heard so much about," he says. "First things first. Are you armed?"

"No."

"Pull up your shirt. Prove it."

Lifting the hem of my shirt up to my ribs, I turn in a slow circle.

"Sorry, I'm afraid that's not good enough. Pull it higher."

I jerk the material up to my armpits and spin until I'm facing him again.

"Are we good?"

"Oh yeah. We're good."

I tug the shirt back down.

"I can see what Jake likes about you. I mean, other than," he gestures at me, waving up and down, which I assume is a reference to my body. "But what do you see in him?"

"Well, for starters, he's never aimed a gun at me."

Garrett laughs. "You're a spitfire."

"You have no idea."

"We could remedy that."

I snort, unable to contain myself. His smile falters.

"Some might consider that a risk," he says.

"If it is, it's one worth taking."

"You're a lot like Janine, aren't you?"

"I'm nothing like Janine."

"I disagree. Say what you will about her, but she isn't afraid to speak her mind, even with a gun aimed at her. And she does whatever it takes to get what she wants."

"Like me dead?" I ask.

He *tsks*. "I can't say I entirely agree with that. Seems like a waste to me."

The man steps out into the light where I can see him. Though he's still cloaked by shadows and half a dozen yards away, I'm shocked by the resemblance between him and Jake, much more obvious in person than it had been in the photograph.

"You know, with Janine gone, I could use a partner."

"Is this a sale's pitch?"

He shrugs.

"More like an offer. A very lucrative one. And considering that accepting it is the only way you're going to walk out of here, it's one that you might want to seriously consider. Assuming you're interested in seeing tomorrow, that is."

Obviously, the time for small talk is over. Which means the time to play the endgame has come.

CHAPTER 37

I pretend to not have heard the threat. Ignore the way the back of my neck prickles like dozens of fire ants have latched on and bitten as I make myself turn my back to him. Take several steps toward the nearest stack of crates.

It's clear by the way the nails have started to rust on the ones with weathered wood, while others are bright and shiny and still smell like pine, that some of the containers are older than others. The dates on the labels affixed to the sides confirm this. I turn back to face him.

"This is a nice place you've got here. Janine must have been stealing for a long time to have gathered so much product."

"I don't know what you're talking about. These containers all hold merchandise for local tourist shops. It's all completely legal."

"I wonder if the cops would agree?"

"Is that your plan? To come here and threaten to turn me in?"

"No. I'm aware that you have people on the inside. Chances are, even if the police seized everything in these crates, you'd have it all back in your possession soon enough."

"You'd be correct about that."

"I know."

"So then why are we here?"

"I came to make you an offer," I say.

He takes another step closer, effectively blocking me off from the door behind him. Lets his eyes slowly drag across my body as he looks me up and down.

"Not that."

His grin, the one that's a bit too much like Jake's, slides off his face. His voice is sharp as he asks, "Then what?"

"I invited you here today to give you a chance to live."

He laughs. "Maybe you aren't as smart as I gave you credit for. In case you haven't noticed, I'm the one with the gun."

"Mmm. True."

"And yet you expect me to take you seriously?"

"I do."

"Even though I could just shoot you now and end this whole thing?"

"Killing me wouldn't solve the problem."

"And how's that?"

"Because if you shoot me, this entire place, and everything in it, goes up in flames."

"How do you figure that?"

Reaching into my pockets, I pull out a glass vial from each and hold them up for him to see. "In one hand, I have some regular old glycerin. In the other, some potassium permanganate. On their own, they're inert.

You can buy them at most hardware stores."

I transfer them both to the same palm and smile.

"But when they're combined, they cause fire."

He points toward the ceiling. "That's why we have a sprinkler system."

"And that's why I picked an accelerant that water will just make worse. And since I have them in these fragile glass containers, should they drop, like if I was injured, well, that would mean we're both in very big trouble."

For the first time, Garrett looks unsure of himself. He shakes his head. "There's no way that's true."

"I'll wait while you google it, if you'd like?"

He pulls his phone from his pocket, glances at the screen, but clearly realizes he'll have to take his attention off me longer than is wise in order to perform the search.

"Yeah, no. I'm calling BS. You're just trying to distract me."

"I assure you, I'm not."

"So I'm just supposed to believe that you know this stuff?"

"You are aware that I've spent the last fifteen years working for the FBI, aren't you?"

The concern creasing his face eases, a small smile appearing on his lips. "So? I've got plenty of friends there. I know that's not something they'd teach you."

"You're right, it's not. But you see, I spent fourteen of those years analyzing data, looking for connections between crimes. That means a lot of reading. A lot of research. I'm sure you heard about the Tampa Torcher. That serial arsonist several years back?"

The way his gaze goes wary, the skin of his throat stretching as he swallows tells me he has.

"Well, I'm the one who discovered the links that

proved the fires were started by the same person. And who was able to predict his next move, enabling the FBI to catch him. Learned all kinds of interesting things in the process. So rest assured when I tell you, if I drop these vials, you're dead."

Pulling at his shirt collar, he says, "There's no way. I mean, if you did that, you'd die first."

"True. But if I don't do something to stop you, I'm dead anyway, right?"

"I'm closer to the door. How do you know I won't escape?"

"You might. From me. But all Janine's hard work here"—he winces as I gesture with the hand holding the vials—"won't. I've already taken the liberty of mailing her a letter letting her know that if this happens, it was your choice. On your watch. And something tells me she won't be too happy with you if this all goes up in smoke."

"What do you want?"

"World peace. But I'll settle for you backing off and making sure Janine does the same. Which means no more snipers. No more hitmen. No more attempts to kill me, or Jake. He and I get to live the remainder of our natural lives together without having to worry about what she's going to try next."

"She won't go for that."

"She's in prison. And I hate to break it to you, but she's going to be there for a very long time. So without someone on the outside to orchestrate things for her and arrange payment, she'll have to."

His lips purse, jaw jutting forward while he thinks. "By the same reasoning, wouldn't that mean I'd be safe from her, as well?"

"No."

"How do you figure that?"

"Because if I die, Jake will take over and do your job for you. Just long enough until you're gone. And I'm betting that with Janine's connections and support that won't take long."

It's a lie. He'd have to know about Garrett's existence and involvement first. But Garrett doesn't need to know that. All he needs to believe is that Janine's insatiable appetite for vengeance might be hereditary.

"And you're just going to take my word for it, if I agree? I simply tell you that you're safe and we both leave here today and go our separate ways?"

"I have several contingency plans already in place. Your car, your home, that cute little restaurant that you're using to launder money… Trust me when I say it will take much longer for you to discover all the little presents I've left for you than Janine's patience will extend."

"How do I know that you won't trigger them anyway, once we leave here?"

"Because I don't want—"

We both freeze, our attention shifting toward the front of the building in unison as a noise comes from outside. Garrett returns his eyes to me, holds a finger up to his lips with one hand while keeping the gun aimed at me with the other as he skitters backward, disappearing into the shadows by the door. A second later, it opens.

And just like that, all my hard work and effort and planning vanish in an instant. I no longer have the upper hand. I no longer have a hand at all. And Garrett knows it.

CHAPTER 38

My stomach clenches as if I've been kicked in the gut. The taste of bile coats the back of my tongue while a wave of horror sweeps over me as I realize how badly I've messed up. I don't think I've ever loathed myself as much as I do in this moment.

Not during the years I spent trapped with my high school boyfriend, Matt, when his sheriff daddy made it clear what would happen if I ended the relationship. Not when I woke up in a serial killer's basement because I foolishly rushed to question him on my own. Not even when I came home after twenty years and realized my grandfather had been murdered, and I'd missed seeing him one last time because of a cowardly fear of my hometown.

The look of relief on Jake's face as he walks through the door is the direct opposite of what must be on mine. As we lock eyes, his expression morphs into confusion. It's clear I'm not happy to see him. But he doesn't know why yet.

I want to scream. Yell for him to run. But I know it wouldn't do any good. He wouldn't leave. Even if I could somehow convince him to, it's too late for that.

"Cassie?"

I wince as he steps farther into the warehouse, silently begging him to stop. And he does. But only when he feels the barrel of the gun against the back of his head.

"Well, now. Isn't this convenient? Here I was, thinking I might be in trouble and now Prince Charming's come to my rescue."

"This doesn't change anything," I say.

"Oh, I think we all know that it does. Unless you want me to shoot him right here so you can watch."

"Whatever you had planned, Cassie, still do it," Jake says.

Garrett jabs the gun into Jake's skull so hard he stumbles forward. The sound of the slide as the man racks a round into the chamber echoes off the walls.

"Stop!" I shout, tears welling in my eyes. "Please. Don't."

"That's what I thought."

"What do you want me to do?" I ask.

"For starters, set one of the vials on that crate beside you."

I do as he says.

"Roll the other one over to me."

Jake gives me a warning look. Mouths *don't*. But what choice do I have? I brought this on us. If something bad happens to him because of that, it will absolutely destroy me. I have to do everything within my power to buy the time to try to get him out of this.

Feeling like a fish that's been gut hooked, sharp barbs tearing at my insides, I bend down, set the glass container on the floor and give it a push. The tube clatters across the concrete, stopping several feet shy of its target. Keeping the gun aimed at Jake, Garrett steps forward and stomps on it.

"Now, then. Where do we go from here? Decisions, decisions."

It's clear from the gleeful smirk Garrett wears that he's enjoying this.

"I think, to start, us guys are going to get out of here for a while. Give you a little time to cool off. But don't worry, I'll be back before you have a chance to miss me. It's just too bad the same can't be said about Loverboy here."

My head's shaking from side to side. My chest is so tight I can barely breathe. If I let that man leave with Jake, I may never see him again.

"You don't—"

"But I do," Garrett cuts me off. "You've been a very ungrateful guest. I want you to think about that while I'm gone. And what you can do to try and make it up to me when I get back."

He gives Jake a shove toward the door, but Jake plants his feet, refusing to leave. I cover my eyes, afraid of what I might see. My voice is thick with grief as I say, "Jake, please. I love you."

His voice is full of defeat as he answers, "I love you too, Cassie. Always have. Always will. You'll find a way to get through this."

But as I lower my hands until our eyes meet, I'm not sure that I will. Because Jake didn't say *we* would get through this. He believes that I alone will survive what happens. And I'm terrified that he might be right.

This is all my fault. If I had told him what I had planned, he wouldn't be here right now. He'd be safe.

Until this moment, this was only about me. I'm the

one Janine wants gone. I'm the one who caused this to happen.

Now, I can only pray that the consequences are mine alone to bear, that Janine's reach will be enough to keep Jake safe. The grin that Garrett gives me as he shoves Jake outside, though, let's me know that it's not.

I'm on my way across the room before the door is even closed. It slams with a deafening bang. I'm close enough to hear the lock click. Grabbing the knob, I give it a twist, but it won't move.

Dropping to my knees, I study the latch. The strike plate has a raised bar, concealing the deadbolt. There's no way to get to it to try and pry it open.

I look around for something to knock the pins on the hinges up, but the only things I see that might work are the nails holding the crates together. Even if I managed to pry one of the crossbars off, I'd have to then get one of the nails out of the wood in order to use it and most appear to have been driven in at an angle. There's no telling how long that might take to do with my bare hands.

I'm trapped. If I don't get out of here, Jake is dead. Even if I do, I have no idea how I'll be able to find him to save him. But one thing at a time.

There are no windows in the building. Just corrugated metal walls. The concrete floor. The ventilation fans on the ceiling, two stories up. My gaze trails from the slowly spinning blades to the towers of crates beneath them.

It's a crazy idea. I'll probably break my neck trying. But what's the alternative? I wait for Garrett to come back and find out what he has in store for me?

I walk over to the highest tower of crates. Try to gauge how far it is from the nearest fan opening. Realize it doesn't really matter and start climbing.

Placing the toe of my tennis shoe on the thin crossbar, I reach up as high as I can. My arms tremble as I pull myself up. My legs do, too. It's a shock to discover how weak my body feels. How quickly fatigue sets in. The way my head begins to throb, my pulse making the tender flesh over my bruised temple ache.

But the pain doesn't make me give up. Instead, it takes my despair and turns it into something else. Fury.

I'm enraged by the men out in the woods. By Garrett. But most of all, by Janine. And the best revenge will be getting out of here and living a long, happy life with her son.

I vow to do exactly that as splinters gouge into my palms. My fingernails bend painfully and break. The rusty head of a nail snags against my shin, tearing my skin open. Each new injury fuels my anger and strengthens my resolve. I *will* get out of here.

There was a time when this climb wouldn't have been a challenge for me. When I would have done it just for kicks. Suddenly, my weight isn't such a heavy burden on my limbs as memories wrap themselves around me, drawing me back into the past.

I'm four years old. Jake and I sit side by side on the branch of an oak, swinging our legs. A warm breeze ruffles the leaves around us. The scents of the swamp, sulfur and sweet grass, tickle my nose.

Tipping my head back, I peer through the branches above us. Jake wraps one of his hands around my arm. Holds onto me as he warns, "Careful."

Shifting my gaze to his, I ask, "What do you think the sky feels like?"

"Like the air around us. It's the same."

Shaking my head, an act that threatens to upset my

balance, causing his grip on me to tighten, I say, "I mean the sky up there." I point toward the patches of blue visible through the canopy above us. "I want to touch it."

"Cassie," he warns.

"I'm going."

"It's too high. It isn't safe."

"Will you come with me?"

I hold out my hand. Jake looks at it for a long minute before he takes it and smiles, revealing his missing front tooth.

"Always."

Pausing on a narrow ledge, I blink back tears from the memory. Shake out my arms and take a couple of deep breaths. Then I continue to climb.

I don't look up. I focus only on my next handhold, my next move, my next step. I can already feel the draft of the fan drying the perspiration on my face.

And then I've done it, found myself on top of the uppermost crate. There's nowhere left to climb.

I lie on my back. Curl my knees to my chest. And kick.

The grate holding the fan in place gives on the first strike. Standing on my toes, I move it aside, then jump. Squirm as I struggle to lift myself through the square-shaped hole, worming my way inch by inch, the edge digging into my chest, then my ribs, then my stomach.

The sun beats down mercilessly as I flop on top of the flat, asphalted roof, panting. Sweat stings my eyes. The heat bakes my skin, wicking what little moisture I retain from my system. I'm out of the warehouse, but now I have a much bigger problem—getting off of it.

CHAPTER 39

There's an old adage about jumping out of the frying pan into the fire. That's exactly what this feels like—being roasted alive. I was already exhausted and dehydrated, but even if I wasn't, it quickly becomes clear that I won't last long up here. Already I feel the last of my strength being zapped away.

Rolling over, I push myself onto my hands and knees. The scorching roof makes my flesh feel like it's melting as I crawl over to the side of the building. A wave of vertigo crashes against me as I look down, making me realize what a horrible idea this was as I feel myself sway, drifting precariously too far over the edge of the building.

Tossing myself back, I collapse onto my side. Squeeze my eyes shut against the dizziness making my head spin. But what I saw is still there, seared onto the backs of my lids. The two stories of metal that separate me from the ground below. But also…

I inch my hand forward, out into the open space.

Stretching as far as I dare, I reach down, over the side of the roof. Slap around blindly until I feel it. A rain gutter is tucked around the ledge of the building. Which means there's at least one downspout around here somewhere.

Keeping my hand on the gutter, I drag myself forward, reaching one corner, then a second, then a third. And there it is.

Lying on my belly, I lean over and look at it. It appears sturdy enough, but will it be able to take my weight? Even if it can, how am I going to climb down it? I've never been scared of heights before, but this is different.

This is—what do they make gutters out of, aluminum? So this would be me basically relying on a soda can to keep myself from crashing to the ground and certain death. My muscles are already fatigued. My grip is already weak. My hopes already dashed. But I wasn't raised to give up.

Butch's voice sounds inside my head, telling me exactly that. While Jake, even as a young child, always encouraged me to be cautious, my grandfather took a different approach.

"You never know if you don't try."

"Where there's a will, there's a way."

"Never let fear stop you from spreading your wings, Cassidy. You were born to fly."

Perhaps it wasn't the soundest advice to give a kid like me, but it gave me the confidence I needed to believe that I could do the impossible. To get up, brush myself off, and try again after every failure, which, considering that those wings of mine have yet to keep me in the air despite all the times I've thrown myself into the void, attempting to soar, were many.

It's never been more important to refuse to quit than

it is right now. And since Jake isn't here to be my voice of reason, it's time to channel that reckless, wild child I was raised to be.

I have everything to lose, but everything means nothing against what I stand to gain.

Pulling my shirt off, I thread it around the downspout and use the material to give a hard tug. It doesn't move. Still on my stomach, I wrap the ends of the fabric around my hands. Then slowly, carefully, I swing my legs over the edge.

That initial moment when my feet are dangling out over space is terrifying. Sweat beads off my face onto the roof in giant splats as I scoot inch by inch until the edge is lodged painfully beneath my bottom rib. Squeezing my legs together, I hold the downspout in a death grip between my knees, take a deep breath, and drop one hand to the pipe.

The splinters embedded in my palms dig deeper as I scrabble for a hold. Black spots pop before my eyes. I'm trembling so hard I feel like I'm convulsing as I push my torso away from the building, knees leveraged against it, until my other hand has no choice but to join the first.

Somehow, I've managed to get on the downspout without falling. Clenching the ends of my shirt in an iron grip, I work my feet flat against the metal wall. Then slowly, step by step, I lower myself down.

I have no clue what I'm going to do once I reach the ground. Get in my car and look for help, but who do I call? The local police? They'd be able to respond the fastest, but can I trust them? What if they're on Janine's payroll? The Miami FBI field office? Garrett himself said he had agents who were friends. Director Jacobson? How long would it take her to send a response?

That's time Jake might not have. Assuming that he's

still alive.

As my feet hit against the crumbling asphalt, it's not tears of relief that blur my vision, but of frustration. What if I've gone through all this for nothing?

But I can't give up. I have to keep going.

I stagger toward the front of the building, pulling my shirt back on. Rounding the corner, I draw to a sudden halt.

Something's missing. A forest-green hatchback, which must be the car Jake used to get here, is parked beside Garrett's convertible. But the white sedan I drove is nowhere to be seen. It's gone.

Of course. I had insinuated that I'd put some kind of explosive on Garrett's Mercedes, an absolutely idiotic move in hindsight. And I'd left my keys in the ignition.

Hurrying over to the hatchback, I try the door. Locked. Framing my face with my hands, I peer through the window. It has a push button ignition. Even if I managed to get inside, it's not going anywhere, not without the key fob.

I turn to face Garrett's Mercedes, a classic from the 60s or 70s. The shiny silver 280SL appears to be in pristine condition. But not for long.

Marching over to the warehouse, I fish my gun from the weeds, then snatch the chunk of concrete from beside the door. Holding it in my fist like a dagger, I approach the vehicle, intending to slash my way through the convertible's soft top, but something on the ground catches my attention first.

Bending, my hand strikes out like a snake, afraid that if I'm not quick enough, it'll disappear. I stare at the device in my palm. It's Jake's burner phone.

The device is scorching hot from baking in the sun. Jagged fissures zigzag across the cracked screen. I hold my breath as I press the button on the side to power it on.

It still works. Not only that, as I take in what I'm looking at, the app that Jake left running, I realize how he knew I was here. And that he must have believed that I'd escape the warehouse to come find him. Any anger I might have felt upon realizing he'd had a tracking device on our car is quickly replaced by hope as I watch the tiny green moving dot.

I jog the remaining steps to Garrett's Mercedes. Use the sharp edge of the concrete to rend a gash through the convertible's top. Reaching through the hole I made, I pop the lock, let myself in, and take a seat behind the wheel. Digging my fingers into the gap on the steering column, I tear it open.

I've just made a wreck of Garrett's car, but that'll be the least of his concerns. In just a few minutes, I'll have this baby hotwired and running. Then, I'm coming for him. This time, I have the element of surprise on my side along with a blinding rage I won't hesitate to use.

I gave him the chance to walk away from this battle. He failed to take it. Now, he'll have to deal with the consequences. As far as I'm concerned, this is war. I might not be able to end it, but for now I'll settle with ending him.

CHAPTER 40

Adrenaline floods my system in steady pulses as I race along US1, weaving in and out of traffic, driving like a maniac. I'm not worried about attracting attention—let the cops try to pull me over. I want them to come after me. Thanks to Jake's tracking app, I'll lead them right to where they need to be.

Only, as I pass a squad car while going fifty miles an hour over the posted speed limit and they fail to give chase, I realize that's not going to happen. Garrett's Mercedes is too distinctive, too easily recognizable. The police don't know that he's not the one behind the wheel. Even if local law enforcement isn't on his side, it appears as if they're not willing to start trouble with him either.

Which means I'm on my own.

A sinking sensation sweeps over me at the thought. Glancing down at the phone screen, I'm hit by another, this one strong enough that I feel myself being pulled down by the undertow. Because that little blinking dot on the screen? It's stopped moving.

Multiple horns honk as I veer into oncoming traffic to pass a dump truck, pulling back into my lane less than a dozen feet before a head-on collision. But it's not the close call that has my heart thumping so hard against the walls of my chest.

I turn off onto a side road, still traveling so fast that I'm practically standing as I jerk the wheel. Glimpses of the ocean ahead appear as I catch air over potholes. Rundown buildings pen me in on the sides, fishing traps and scrapped boats littering the patchy dirt yards.

According to the tracker app, I'm getting close to where the car Jake and Garrett were in has stopped. I'm forced to slow, afraid that I'll miss a turn, but even as I do, I know it's in vain. The tension in my gut tells me where they've gone. And as I spot the white sedan parked ahead, my suspicions are confirmed.

Coming to a stop, I debate my options. As I watch the two figures get farther away down the pier, I know I don't have long to make my decision. Horror swells inside my chest as I realize I'm out of time—and so is Jake.

Hopping out of the car, I break into a run, moving as fast as my legs will carry me. The two men in front of me have come to a stop. The smaller of the two gestures. The larger moves to the very edge of the crumbling wooden structure.

They're at least two hundred feet away, too far for them to hear the sound of my shoes slapping against the blacktop. But not too far for me to see the dejected slump of Jake's shoulders as he turns his back to the other man, facing the water.

I reach the sedan just as Jake laces his hands together, placing them on the top of his head. I stretch my arms across the top of the car. Try desperately to control my breathing as Jake sinks down, one knee making contact with the dock.

In this moment, I couldn't care less about any oath I've taken to uphold the law. Or about following protocol. Screw the book. I don't announce myself. I don't say a word. As Jake's second knee approaches the wood, I curl my finger, a gentle squeeze, not a pull, timed with my exhale.

Jake's body jerks as a series of gunshots ring out. A flock of seagulls takes to the air with startled cries. The earth seems to shake beneath my feet, my shoes thudding hollowly across the deck as I run, blinded by tears as I sob uncontrollably.

Then I'm in the air, a pair of strong arms wrapped around me so tightly my ribs feel like they might snap, but I don't care about that, or the way I can't breathe, or the sudden overwhelming urge I have to pee. All I care about is the mouth pressed against mine.

"Are you okay?" I ask, pulling back, inspecting Jake's body from head to toe as I squeeze his cheeks between my hands so hard that I might leave bruises.

"I'm fine. What about you?"

I answer him with a series of kisses as I do my best to cover every inch of his face, not stopping until we're both breathless. Squeezing my eyes shut, I lean against his chest, listening to the beat of his heart beneath my ear. I'm not sure I've ever heard such a beautiful sound before.

"It's over," I sigh.

"Is it?" he asks, stroking my head.

I know what he's asking—not just about the events of this day, but everything that led us here. I debate briefly before saying, "I think things should be quiet for at least the next week."

He chuckles. "Then we should go out to dinner tonight, get some champagne."

I shake my head no.

"Then what do you want to do to celebrate?"

I lean back until I can see him.

"Have a picnic," I say, knowing that this time when I fall asleep in his arms in front of the wall of glass, I'll wake up in them, too.

The grin he gives me makes everything we just went through worth it. His eyes flick toward the main road, where the sound of sirens in the distance grows louder as they approach.

"Maybe we should have a quick pre-game celebration now. Once they get here, I doubt we'll be going anywhere for a while."

I try giving him a look of disapproval, but I can't keep my lips from spreading into a smile. He's not wrong. And for me, he'll always be Mr. Right.

CHAPTER 41

The room is uncomfortably cold. Every part of me aches. And now that my adrenaline has worn off, I'm having trouble keeping my eyes open. I slide off the uncomfortable metal chair and onto Jake's lap, ignoring the raised eyebrows given to me by the two detectives across from us.

I don't care what they think as I nestle against his chest, absorbing his warmth. Relishing the feeling of being cradled in his embrace. Let them stare. We came way too close to never being able to do this again. Besides, in another ten minutes, his arms might be the only thing keeping me upright.

The woman shifts her weight. "We spoke with your director. She's confirmed all the background information you've given us. Everything up until you came to the Keys." She shoots her partner a look, then says, "That's when things get a bit… murky."

I remain silent as I return her gaze.

Clearing her throat, she continues. "For starters,

we'd like to know what brought you here to the Keys in the first place."

"Did Director Jacobson tell you about the sniper who took a shot at me?"

"She did."

"He was paid from an account traced to one of your local banks. The inmate who killed Tony Bianchi was as well."

The detectives exchange a long look. "May I ask which law enforcement agency is conducting that investigation?"

Shrugging, I say, "As far as I'm aware, none of them."

She frowns, eyes narrowing. Crosses her arms over her chest as she leans back in her seat while her partner takes over the questioning.

"So none of this information was obtained through official channels?"

"It was not."

His tone is disapproving as he says, "That seems to be a common thread with you, Agent Knox."

"How so?"

"Why didn't you call the local authorities and inform them of what was going on?"

"I was busy." When his expression makes it clear he isn't satisfied with that answer, I sigh heavily and add, "And also, no offense, but I don't trust any of you."

The woman chokes on the sip of coffee she just took, turning her head as she coughs the liquid back up. "Excuse me?"

"Garrett implied that he had cops on his payroll. Feds, too."

"And you believed him?"

"Considering that I went over ninety miles an hour

across two separate Keys and passed at least one squad car that didn't bother to pursue—while I was driving Mr. Glover's extremely recognizable vintage Mercedes—I figured that he was probably telling the truth. But if you'd like to offer another explanation, I'm all ears."

This time, when the two detectives exchange a look, they hold a silent conversation. The man stands, walking across the room. Once his head is blocking the camera mounted in the corner, the woman turns off the recorder on the table.

"We are aware that there are certain… issues within the department. But rest assured, those issues don't extend to either of us."

She rewinds the tape. Plays it forward until my voice says, "I was busy." Giving me a tight smile, she presses record again, effectively wiping my accusation from the record. Her partner bows his back like he just got up to stretch, then returns to his seat.

It's not the smartest move on their part. Both the time of the audio recording and the video will be noted in the case file. Anyone paying attention will notice the discrepancy. But I'm not going to point that out. I've reached my quota of risks for the day.

"Now, then. How did you come to be aware that Garrett Glover was somehow involved in the attempt on your life?"

"Don Farris—that's the hitman—his wife's Facebook page. I scrolled through the pictures in her feed. When I saw one of Don with Garrett, I took a screenshot and ran a reverse image search using Google Lens to find out who he was."

"But how did you know to do that? Did you recognize him?"

This time, I'm the one to shift uncomfortably. "Yes

and no." Lifting my head from Jake's chest, I look him in the eyes. "He bore enough of a resemblance to Jake that I suspected they must be related somehow."

Jake's arms tighten around me.

The female detective says, "That's right. It's your mother who was responsible for ordering the hit."

"Yes," he admits.

"Man. My mother-in-law hates me, but I suppose I should consider myself lucky that she's never taken things that far." She laughs at her own joke, but she's the only one. Realizing that it's fallen flat, she quickly continues, "How did you find the warehouse?"

"I searched his name on the Monroe County Property Tax website. It was one of the addresses listed in his name."

"And you decided to pay it a visit?"

If the tattooed teller from the bank didn't report the actions I took to contact Garrett and get him to meet me there, I'm not going to admit to it now, so I just nod.

"Our crime scene analysts recovered a couple of substances they've yet to identify at that scene. I don't suppose you could help us out with that?"

I grimace. "Glycerin and potassium permanganate. When you combine them, they create fire."

"A bomb?" the man says, his voice rising a couple octaves.

"No, just a chemical reaction between two substances. It was my insurance policy to make sure I'd get out of there okay, though I may have embellished what would happen when they mix. Made him think the reaction would be a bit more sudden and disastrous."

"So what happened? What went wrong?"

"I showed up," Jake says.

"How'd you know where to go? Did Agent Knox

tell you?"

"I did not. He put a tracking device on our car," I say, cutting my eyes at him.

"Are you in the habit of tracking your girlfriend like that, Mr. Walker?" the woman asks, voice dripping with disapproval.

"No."

"You realize that's illegal, don't you? Using an electronic device to determine someone's location without their consent?"

"Yes, ma'am."

"And yet you did it anyway?"

"Jake has my consent to do what he needs to in order to make himself feel better about my profession," I say, interrupting before he can respond.

"But this wasn't part of your job."

"Or about my occasionally reckless behavior," I amend. "And it's a good thing he did, because that's how I found him and Garrett when I escaped the warehouse."

"How did you get out, anyway?" Jake asks.

"Through one of the fans in the ceiling."

Shaking his head, he leans forward and presses a kiss against my temple. Gives the detective a look that clearly asks if she now understands why he might have put a tracking device on our car, but she doesn't seem to notice. She's staring at me with her eyes bugged wide, mouth slightly open.

"You're not kidding, are you?" her partner asks.

"No."

"How did you get down?"

"Gutter downspout."

Now he's giving me a strange look, too. His gaze flicks to Jake with an expression that makes it clear that he, at least, gets the reason behind Jake's action.

"So explain to us what happened when you got down?"

"I saw that Garrett had taken my car, so I hotwired his and took it."

"And you knew where they were going because of the tracking device?"

"Yes. Jake had dropped his phone so I could find it. Left the tracker app open so I'd know what to do."

"You had a phone?" the woman asks in a thready voice.

"Yes."

"Agent Knox, I feel obligated to tell you that next time, instead of going rogue, I highly suggest that you go through official channels."

"Thank you, Detective. I will," I assure her, with a smile and a lie.

She nods. "That brings us to what happened at the marina." Her mouth twists in a knot like she doesn't like the taste of what she has to say next. "Our techs found four bullet casings at the scene."

"Yes."

"We've been asked to check—why so many?"

"I was trained not to pause fire to reassess the situation if the suspect still appears to present a threat."

"As were we. And that was quite a distance you made the shots from. I'm assuming you gave a verbal warning?"

"Of course she did," Jake says before I can answer.

"You see, we have to ask because the medical examiner's preliminary examination indicates that all four shots struck the suspect in the side of the head. Typically, if you've made your presence known and given a warning, the suspect won't be in full profile. There will be some sign, whether they were in the act of turning or whatnot, to signify that they heard someone yelling at them to stop."

I shrug. "I don't know what to tell you."

She gives me a hard look, her eyes boring into mine as she studies me. Finally, she sighs and taps the notepad in front of her. "These are the best numbers to reach the two of you?"

"Yes."

"Then you're free to go."

The tape recorder clicks off. Jake and I stand. As we move to the door, her voice rings out behind us, "Agent Knox?"

I turn back to face her, eyebrows raised. "You did good work here. Made our town a little bit safer and I want to thank you for that. But you should know that chances are you've upset some very dangerous people. The trouble might not be over."

"It never is," I say, and head out the door.

Wrapping an arm around me, Jake guides me through the station and out to the parking lot. Once we're outside, he says, "I can't believe you climbed out through the roof."

"I can't believe you put a tracking device on the car."

He gives me that grin of his, his hand lowering from my waist to my hip. "I'll gladly accept whatever punishment you feel fits the crime."

"Since it all worked out in the end, I won't go too hard on you."

I laugh at his expression of mock disappointment.

Turning serious, he says, "There's just one thing I don't understand."

"What's that?"

He glances over his shoulder, checking that no one

is within hearing distance.

"Why didn't you save yourself all that trouble and just kill him in the first place?"

"I don't kill for sport, Jake. It's not something that I enjoy doing."

"I know, but still…"

Exhaling loudly, I confess, "From the pictures I found online, it was clear that the two of you were related, but I wasn't sure how. Until I got to the warehouse and saw him in person and was able to gauge his age, I thought maybe he could have been your brother."

"He was my uncle," Jake says. "Though I hadn't seen him in decades, since before my mom left. But even if he'd been some sibling I never knew about, I'd still choose you, Cassie. Always will."

"But you don't *have* to choose," I say. "That's what I've been trying to get you to understand. I don't want you to. Even normal families are complicated. If you want to see—or support—either of your parents, then please do. I know it doesn't mean you love me any less."

He stops and pulls me to him. As he gives me a kiss that makes my knees weak and my toes curl, I tell myself that I meant what I just said. Which I do. There just needs to be some ground rules first. But not with him.

Janine's in store for a little visit. And honestly? I can't help kind of looking forward to it.

CHAPTER 42

It's clear the instant she steps into the room and her eyes land on me, the pleasant expression pasted on her face morphing into an angry scowl, that I'm not who she was expecting. She looks past me and scans the room, checking to see who else has come to visit her, but there is no one else. Not Jake, not her lawyer—only me.

The moment she realizes that her mask slips. There's a flash of disappointment. A brief hint of regret. Both are quickly replaced by the unmistakable stoniness of hatred. She sets her jaw and lifts her head, her nose wrinkling in disgust as she takes a step toward me, then hesitates.

For a moment, I think she's going to turn around. Deny the visit and return to her cell. My smile broadens, becomes almost mocking, and she makes her decision. In the end, I guess her curiosity wins out. Or maybe she just wants a break from that six-by-eight foot cage they keep her locked in. Either way, the result is the same.

"What are *you* doing here?" she snarls as she drops

heavily into the seat across from me. The legs scrape loudly across the concrete floor, earning her a glance of disapproval from one of the guards stationed nearby.

"I thought it was time for us to have a little chat, Janine." Her eyes widen as they spot the ring I wear—the one that Jake gave me. It would be kind of hard for her not to see it, since I purposely raised my left hand to fiddle with the collar of my T-shirt for that very purpose. "Or should I call you Mom?"

"That will never happen," she hisses.

"Okay," I say cheerily. "Janine it is, then."

"Where's Jake?"

"At home."

"So, what? You're keeping him away from me now?"

"Not at all. Whether he chooses to visit you or not is completely up to him."

"The only visitors I'm allowed are lawyers and immediate family."

"I know."

"Then how'd you get in here?"

"Oh, I have my ways."

Until this point, her gaze has been glued to my ring, but now, she looks up at me with something like fear. Good.

"You should leave," she snaps.

She twists in her seat, looking for the guard.

"It's in your best interest to hear me out first before I do."

Her head jerks back around.

"Is that a threat?"

"No. But this is. This little vendetta you have against me? It ends. Now."

Rolling her eyes, she huffs a small laugh. "And if it

doesn't?"

"I'm serious, Janine. I'm giving you one warning. You're going to want to take it."

"No." She smirks, shaking her head. "I don't think that I do."

"That's your choice. But I want you to think about how easy it was for me to get in here. And if I can get in to talk to you, I can get in to talk to your fellow prisoners."

"So?"

"You seem like the kind of woman who might have a hard time making friends. Actually, you seem like the type who might have a whole cellblock of inmates you've rubbed the wrong way. I'm sure one of them would be more than happy to take care of you for an extra couple of jars of peanut butter in their account at the canteen."

She swallows hard and my smile grows.

"Obviously, we're never going to be friends," I continue. "But trust me when I say that you do *not* want me as an enemy."

"You're a Fed. You wouldn't dare do anything like that to me."

"Oh, wouldn't I?"

Leaning across the table, I lower my voice. "I've already had to cross a couple of lines I never intended to because of you. I won't hesitate to cross another. Turns out, it gets a little easier each time, which is good, because I fully intend to enjoy a long, happy life with Jake. No matter what I have to do to get that chance."

"I'm not afraid of you."

"As long as you leave me alone, you don't have to be."

With that, I stand to leave. Pause just as I'm passing

her, as if I've been struck by an afterthought.

"I almost forgot. If you *are* stupid enough to keep this little… whatever it is, going, you're going to have to find someone new to do your dirty work for you. Garrett's retired."

Bending at the waist, I whisper in her ear, "I'm afraid I had to kill your poor brother. And you better be glad that I did, because he was seconds away from murdering your son. But, I'm willing to let you live as long as you play nice."

I press a noisy kiss against her cheek and straighten. Look down into her terrified eyes.

"For now," I say, wiggling my finger in a wave. With that, I walk out of the room.

Would I really cross the line of having her killed? I'm not sure. Who knows what we're capable of, until we're pushed to that point. I'd like to think I'd find another way of neutralizing her as a threat. A better way.

But what I do know is that if it does come to that, it's got to be me who does it, not Jake. His mother has already caused him enough heartache for this lifetime.

And Janine? Well, if she decides to take this that far, I'll make sure she has the chance to see it coming. Even if I have to hold her eyes open myself.

CHAPTER 43

The sound of steps comes up quickly behind me. It's nothing that I haven't been expecting. Drawing a deep breath, I turn to face them. Sink to my knees, open my arms wide, and accept my fate. Brace myself for the impact that comes a second later.

Stephano is practically frantic as he climbs up me, his tiny hooves digging into my thighs and gouging at my chest until I swoop him up into a cuddle. He nuzzles my neck, then drags his sandpaper tongue across my cheek as I whisper to him, holding him tight.

Rocky struts up to us and studies me with an orange eye, but it holds none of the fiery contempt that it used to. He even gives my knee an experimental peck, which feels like the bird equivalent of a pat on the back. I can't help but smile.

The pygmy goat and rooster aren't the only ones to show me extra love since my return. Daisy hasn't missed an opportunity to nuzzle her zebra head against me and Charlie, her foal, has taken to mouthing me so much that she gave my leg a hickey. Even Sam Mule has been less cranky, his oversized ears perked in my direction instead of pinned back away from me.

Hal, Jake's head of security at Myers and Kleinman, did a good job taking care of all the animals while we were away. Their bellies were full, waters were filled, and stalls were spotless. But over the last week that we've been back, based on how attention starved they've all acted, it's clear that the man was a bit short on affection.

Or maybe they just missed me that much. Either way, it's almost enough to make me feel bad about those extra few days that Jake and I spent down in the Keys. Almost, but not quite, because the only way to describe those days is magical.

Long walks on the beach, amazingly delicious meals, swimming in the warm, crystal-clear aqua waters… and falling asleep every night in front of our honeymoon suite's wall of glass, wrapped in each other's arms. There's no denying that after everything we've been through lately, we needed the time to relax.

And to reconnect. Which we did, seizing the opportunity to lose ourselves in each other for a while before returning to the reality of our normal lives. Now, we're back to the daily grind. Everything feels the same, yet at the same time, so very different.

Something's shifted between us. The little niggling doubts that once festered in the dark corners of my mind have been silenced. What we have between us somehow feels more permanent, and it's not just because of the ring I still wear on my finger.

As if summoned by my thoughts, Jake's voice breaks through my reverie.

"Cheating on me again, I see," he says, lips pursed

in a mock pout.

"Oh please. Like you're one to talk."

I gesture to the raccoon draped around his neck like a fur stole.

"I'll have you know that Ricki is a lady. She keeps her touches appropriate. Unlike that little horned deviant."

I glance down at the muddy hoofprints smeared across the front of my shirt and smirk. "You're just jealous."

"Darn right I am."

I give Stephano a gentle squeeze before setting him down. As I stand, brushing myself off, I watch him frolic over to where Rocky's scratching at the dirt. He prances a tight circle around the rooster until the bird raises his head, bobbing it, the two engaging in their own very bizarre version of dancing.

"You'll get your turn," I promise.

"Yeah?" Jake asks.

He lifts the raccoon from around his neck and sets her on top of Chip and Bagel's stall door. The kit scampers down into the stall, where one of the pigs gives a squeal of glee at the arrival of their new friend. It's odd, the matches that are made in the animal kingdom. But are those made between humans any less strange?

"Yeah."

"How about now?" he suggests, his voice low and husky.

"Here?"

He gives me that grin I can't resist.

"Have you done all your chores?" I ask, taking a step closer to him.

"No."

I put my hand on his chest. "Neither have I."

"I guess that means it's going to be a late night."

Gathering a fistful of his shirt, I pull him toward me. Hold his gaze as I start walking backward, tugging him with me toward the tack room.

"Or an early morning," I counter.

"Sleep's overrated, anyway."

He loops his arms around me, pulling me close. Gives me a kiss that's electric. I feel safe, and happy, and loved. I feel home. I've never had my life flash before my eyes, but if it ever does? These are the moments that I want to remember.

OTHER BOOKS BY SHANNON

CASSIDY KNOX SERIES:

Deadly Sanctuary
Fatal Betrayal
Grave Waters
Bitter Truth

CHIEF MAGGIE RILEY SERIES:

The Girl Who Lied
Their Angel's Cry
The Shadow Girl
One Little Sigh
The Day She Died
Her Broken Dreams

PSYCHOLOGICAL THRILLERS:

Best Friends Forever
The Slumber Party
Would You Rather
Her Hiding Place

READER'S NOTE

Dear Reader,

A huge and most sincere THANK YOU for choosing to read BITTER TRUTH, the fourth book in the Cassidy Knox series! With so many books out there to choose from, you have no idea how much it means to me that you chose to spend some of your precious reading time with one of mine, so I have to say it again—THANK YOU!!!!

Not only did this book allow me to share two of my favorite places—the Florida Everglades AND the Florida Keys—but while visiting the Keys while writing this one, I got to see some of the elusive Keys deer! It took me years to find some, and I'm still over the moon about it! If you ever get the chance to visit either place, I highly recommend you seize it (but trust me… do it in the winter).

If you enjoyed BITTER TRUTH, I'd be so very grateful if you took the time to leave a rating and/or a review. Even just a few words can have a huge impact on helping other readers find and choose to read it as well, which would be amazing because I love everything about this series and want to keep bringing it to you for a long time. I can't wait for you to find out what I have in store for Cassidy and Jake!

If you'd like to keep up with my latest book news and releases, please consider following me on Amazon or BookBub. Even better, sign up for my monthly newsletter via my website at www.shannonhollinger.com where you can enter to win signed books, find out about contests for additional prizes, make your voice heard by voting on cover designs, titles, etc., become an ARC reader, and so much more! (Your email address will never be shared, and you can unsubscribe at any time.)

Thank you again for your support—it really is hugely appreciated!

Until next time,

Shannon Hollinger

ACKNOWLEDGEMENTS

First, I'd like to thank Chazzie Ann Chaney and Linda Cunningham, winners of the "name the raccoon" contest! They're responsible for giving Ricki her name—a giant thank you, ladies!

As always, a huge thank you to alpha reader Kaycee Racer. She's been with Cassidy from the start, and she always knows just what the story needs to make it better. You can find her at www.retrospect-publishing.com.

A heartfelt thank you to my amazing friend Maureen Downey (@booklovermo525) for beta reading (even though Jake pissed you off).

Thank you to friend and proofreader Melissa Ammons and her "eagle eyes." You can find Melissa at www.melissaproofs.com.

Thank you to all my wonderful ARC readers for your early reviews! You have no idea how much I appreciate those of you who show up every single time for every single book. You guys are the best!

Thank you to my mom, Stacy, for instilling in me an almost obsessive love of reading from an early age. The summer reading lists she made me exposed me to books I never would have read, worlds I wouldn't have experienced, and characters I still haven't forgotten.

To my dad, Bob, who never got to see me achieve my dreams, but always believed I would one day. Thank you for never doubting me. I miss you.

To my grandmother, Marvis. Thank you for introducing me to the work of so many dark, twisty, and unforgettable authors! There are so many amazing books I would never have discovered without you!

Thank you to my husband, Ben, for all the adventures. We've hiked thousands of miles together, from Florida to Maine and many states in between, during which I've pointed out all the best places to hide a body, and yet he still never hesitates to hit the trail with me, even when he knows I've got murder on my mind. That's love!

My endless gratitude to all the readers, reviewers, librarians, booksellers, Bookstagrammers BookTokers, and everyone else out there who takes the time to share your love of books! You all deserve something special, so go ahead and get that new book you've got your eye on! What the heck—get two! Or ten!

And most importantly, a big, huge, giant THANK YOU to you, reader! Your support means the absolute world to me, and I'm so incredibly grateful for each and every single one of you who chooses to spend some of your precious reading time with one of my books! I can never thank you enough for that!

Reviews are the most important gift you can give an author, so if you enjoyed your time with this book, please consider leaving a few words, or even just a rating, to help other readers find it as well! Thank you!

ABOUT THE AUTHOR

With degrees in Crime Scene Technology and Physical Anthropology, Florida writer Shannon Hollinger hasn't just seen the dark side of humanity—she's been elbow deep inside of it! She's an avid animal lover, reader, and hiker, and has been known to use her forensic skills to figure out who ate the last cookie in the house.

A multi-genre, Amazon charts best-selling author, Shannon writes psychological thrillers filled with jaw-dropping twists and shocking endings, the police procedural Chief Maggie Riley mysteries, where the darkness of the Maine wilderness is rivaled only by the deadly secrets it conceals, and the romantic suspense Cassidy Knox mystery thrillers, where the animals will steal your heart and the nights are as hot as the days.

Her novels have been translated into multiple languages, and her short fiction has appeared in *Suspense Magazine*, *Mystery Weekly*, and *The Saturday Evening Post*, among many other magazines and anthologies.

Shannon is a member of the International Thriller Writers and the Short Mystery Fiction Society.

To keep current on book news and to enter monthly giveaways, contests, become an ARC reader, and more, sign up for Shannon's newsletter through her website at **www.shannonhollinger.com.**

Find Shannon on social media:

Facebook	@thiswritersays
Instagram	@thiswritersays
BookBub	@shannonhollinger
TikTok	@shannonhollinger
Pinterest	@thiswritersays

Made in the USA
Coppell, TX
14 June 2026

79107285R10152